Praise for *The Amazing Twin Chicken Freedom Fighters*

"There's a beautiful energy to *The Amazing Twin Chicken Freedom Fighters,* a verve reminiscent of Manuel Gonzalez's *The Regional Office is Under Attack* and Kurt Vonnegut's *Slaughterhouse-Five*. If you must know anything about this novel before you get to it, know this: Zephaniah Sole's voice has an outrageous authority that commands your attention and rattles your imagination."

—Juan Carlos Reyes, author of *Three Alarm Fire*

"Zephaniah Sole has created an entertaining, high-action absurdist romp that grabs the reader in its teeth and does not let up. It's bewildering and engaging and entirely sui generis. This is a fearless novel and a hell of a lot of fun to read."

—Cari Luna, author of *The Revolution of Every Day*

"Nothing as batshit crazy, surreal, absurd, or just plain weird as *The Amazing Twin Chicken Freedom Fighters* has any business feeling so genuine and so real. It might just be the perfect book for our times."

—Joey R. Poole, author of *I Have Always Been Here Before*

"Meta dialogue, political commentary, and clever puns abound in this fast-paced story. Zephaniah Sole's novel unfolds like an uneasy dream, as the protagonists find themselves transformed—into chickens. Something's foul, fowl, (and awfully funny)."

—Allison Whittenberg, author of *Sweet Thang*

"*The Amazing Twin Chicken Freedom Fighters* is the deep, learned, bookish, illogical, profound, effervescent, scatological, otherworldly, etymological and hilarious history of a shift in Joy's and Jake's (not their real names) ways of being and ours after they leap as one from a bridge and become heroic, pizza-eating—not just any pizza, but The Pizza Eternal—soul-yoked chickens. Enchanters, clicking and singing cetacean metaphors, the-down-and-out, lambs, assassins, the sorrowful, the faceless, the brain-on-fire, the ego-mad, the blind and seers inhabit Sole's audacious and ambitious soul-adventure. This is a wild novel as sweet and hot as a from-the-oven lemon rosemary scone. Onward to Book Two."

—Jo Perry, author of *Everything Happens*, *Pure*, and *The World Entire*

Editor: Krysta Winsheimer of Muse Retrospect

Cover design: Garth Jackson

ISBN: 979-8-9904851-2-9
Run Amok Books, 2025
First Edition

RunAmok

Printed in the USA

THE AMAZING TWIN CHICKEN FREEDOM FIGHTERS

ZEPHANIAH SOLE

Para Luz, la Alegría de mi inspiración.

CHAPTER 1

There was a bridge.

An art deco bridge. With truss arches built in 1937, spanning 4,200 and, no… It was a neo-Gothic cable-stayed/suspension bridge built in 1883, spanning 1,590… no… no… It was of reddish-orange hue and built in 1913. With a double-leaf, Rall-type bascule lift spanning 270… It doesn't matter.

There was a bridge.

The bridge was long and the bridge was high and below the bridge was the water. And the water below was clean and cold and… No, it wasn't. It was polluted with human waste and hypodermic needles. Doesn't matter. The water matters: a tributary marching toward its main stem river. And the water was being looked at. Observed. Perceived. By a man.

There was a man.

The man stood on the bridge and watched the water below. Nope. That's a lie. He wasn't watching the water. It was night. He wouldn't have been able to see it clearly. Besides, when we curse G_d, we tend to look up.

So the man unleashed a stream of profanities toward the sky. Then he swung a leg over the pedestrian guardrail and straddled it. For some reason, he thought to check the time. His Fitbit said 11:11 p.m. This served no purpose for him, but it does for us. We now have a general idea of when this all occurs, occurred, will occur… Fitbits didn't hit the market until the twenty-first century, right?

"Whiskey, tango, foxtrot," muttered the man. A lovely little phrase with an idiosyncratic origin that hints at his background and general character. The time brought to mind the symbolism he'd encountered earlier that day. We'll come back to that in a bit, the symbolism fit in by the Fitbit. For now, the man swung his other leg over the rail and stepped onto the thin concrete platform that jutted out just far enough to let him balance his body on his heels. He faced the open air and leaned back on the rail and felt the chaotic wind beckon him to…

"What! The. Ever-loving. *Fuck!*" a rather shrill voice screamed from behind.

Using the rail for support, he rotated his body. Across the traffic lanes, holding the guardrail on the opposite side of the bridge, was a woman.

There was a woman.

And the woman screamed, "You are fucking up my GCW!"

Let's pause for a moment and talk about this woman.

(Flashback!)

***

Earlier that night, at approximately 9:16 p.m. or 10:23 p.m. or 8:49 p.m., the woman sat at the small circular desk in the kitchen of her 489-square-foot studio apartment and completed her suicide letter. Said letter read as such:

Tiberius laughed.

Peering at the woman from the conceit of his throne, he laughed and the court laughed and the woman set her face and prayed.

"If he's still alive..." Tiberius roared, "... there's no way... I mean, come on, lady, you were there, you saw the whole... What with the knives and the whips and the rope and... ?"

The woman pulled an egg from her skirt and held it for all to see.

"Chances of that guy still being alive?" Tiberius continued. "If I was a betting man, which I'm not, but say I was? I'd quicker bet money on that egg, right here, right now, turning red."

And here, Mamá, you would kiss the top of my head. I already knew how the story ended. You'd tell it to me over and over again, especially whenever it was getting close to my birthday. I always had the same question. "What was inside the egg?"

"That's why you were born on Easter, pollita," you'd say. "You have to go out into the world and find out."

But all I've found is pain. And fear. And great, great loneliness. And I know, Mamá, you will be so disappointed in me, but I'm sorry. I cannot take this loneliness anymore.

I'm sorry.

-JOY

***

The man looked at his Fitbit again. 11:12 p.m. See how the

Fitbit is useful? It brought us back into the present moment that happened in the past but not as deep in the past as the past we were… whatever… "What's a GCW?" the man shouted across the bridge to the woman.

"What?"

"What's. A. *G. C. W*?"

The woman gripped the rail on her side with one hand and touched her fingers to her temple with the other as if indicating the answer was obvious. "Goodbye, Cruel World," she shouted back.

The man climbed back over the rail to the safe side of the pedestrian platform. "That's not a thing. You just made that up."

"That's not a…" The woman screwed up her face. "Any word or phrase for anything anywhere is something someone made up! Everyone makes everything up. Why can't I?"

A car zoomed between them. "I didn't mean…" the man said.

"You should mean! Everything you say should mean without being mean!"

"Look, I didn't mean to screw up your GCW."

"No breaking eggs today."

"I'm sorry?" the man asked, overwhelmed now with nausea.

"Don't be sorry, just come back another day."

"No, I mean…"

"Don't be mean!"

"I'm not being mean, I *meant*, what did you say before?"

"Before what?"

***

You see, that morning, at approximately 10:05 a.m. or 9:21 a.m. or 11:17 a.m., the man began his morning as he began every morning—staring into eyes reflected back at him from his broken, foggy bathroom mirror. Dark brown eyes, hidden behind condensation and bits of food flung from daily flossing. Eyes that refused to flinch as he pulled the trigger to the .40-caliber Glock 22 he'd pressed against his right temple.

He pulled the trigger slow, and he pulled the trigger smooth, back, back, until he heard the click of the released firing pin. The tameness of that click was all he ever heard. He never loaded the weapon.

Okay, he thought—taking his eyes off his eyes and placing the weapon on top of his toilet bowl tank—time for breakfast.

He went from the bathroom to the kitchenette of his mold-odored, low-ceilinged "apartment" in the basement of his landlord's two-story Victorian home and pulled out a dwindled stick of butter and one very last egg from the carton in his sparsely populated refrigerator. He warmed up his nonstick pan on his electric hot plate, plopped in the rest of his butter, and cracked open the egg.

When he looked at the pan was the first time he felt nauseous that day, the third time being later that night when he spoke with the woman on the bridge. There were two yolks in the pan, simmering. The man had heard of this phenomenon but had never directly observed it. Which is understandable. Though there are reports of individuals frequently cracking open double-yolked eggs for their morning meals, the odds of it occurring are approximately one in one thousand. This is better than the chances of being struck by lightning (one in three thousand) or winning most state and national lotteries (between one in one hundred thousand and one in fifteen million). But still, it's pretty rare.

The man flung the pan off the hot plate. It clattered against the wall of his kitchenette, and yolks and albumen dripped down the tiles like the snot of a sick child.

***

"Before what?" the woman shouted across the bridge again.

"Nothing," the man said. "I'm just hungry. Why are you doing this?"

The woman shook her head as if saying "no," and the dark strands of her bob-cut hair tumbled over her face. She held up a palm like a traffic cop. "Come back another day."

"Why are you—" he pressed.

"Why are you?" she shot back.

He massaged the back of his neck. "I'm useless."

The woman brushed the hair from her face. "Is your mind made up?"

"Yeah."

"My mind is made up."

"Okay."

"I am going," she shouted.

"I'll go with you."

She let out a nervous laugh. "You'll… ?"

"Yeah."

She gripped the rail on her side. Another car zoomed between them. "Come on, then."

"Let's go from my side."

"My side's better," she said.

"Mine is."

"You can see more city lights from my side!"

"That's exactly what I don't want to see," he shouted back.

"I want to see the lights!"

"To remind you of all the shit that brought you here?"

The woman climbed over the rail onto the pedestrian platform. "Let's meet in the middle."

"The what?"

"The middle!"

"The middle?"

"Yes!" the woman said. "You speak English?"

The man chuckled. When the woman said "middle" it sounded like "meedle."

"If we meet in the meedle…" he poked fun.

"Don't"—she cut him off with another traffic-cop palm and a surprisingly cold glare—"make fun of my accent. I bet I know *way* more English than you."

"Probably," the man conceded. "But that ain't saying much."

The woman stepped over a lower guardrail between the steel beams of a truss and went out into the vehicle lanes of the bridge.

"Just meet in the middle," she said.

***

The man does not have a car. Earlier that day, he took the subway to get to the... no, no, that's always the problem, there's no subway where he lives, there's a subway where he *used* to live, but now he has to take a train called the MAX, but out of habit he still calls it the subway and, hey, this is... We can do whatever we want. Let's call it the subway. The man took the subway to get to the bridge. Or did he walk? He took the subway. Yes. He emerged from his basement apartment by way of the separate entrance at the side of the house, breathed in the spring air, and walked past the front porch of the Victorian home, where his landlord lounged on a wicker sofa, beamed a Botox smile, and said, "Lovely evening for a walk."

The man waved, not breaking stride. "Yes, sir, it is."

The Landlord said something back but the man didn't hear. He was already hightailing it down the street, and in short order, made it to the subway station a mere two or three or seven blocks away. He descended a stairwell and could already hear the cries of the Vagrant echoing off the subterranean walls:

"Got to come down here to hear. But I know you can!"

The Vagrant's words grew louder as the man paid his fare and passed through the turnstile... There're no turnstiles here... Doesn't matter, we can do whatever we want... The man passed through the turnstile and walked down another flight of stairs, and the Vagrant's words grew even louder:

"Them Enchanters were never defeated! Not since the first one en español!"

The man stepped out onto the subway platform. He could see the Vagrant now, posted at his usual location. "They in them monkeys, screaming on your shoulders! In them faceless things! In them advertisements!"

Everyone else ignored the Vagrant, but the man listened.

"Want to have a full life? Eat McDonald's! Want to have best friends? Wear Levi's! Want to fall in love? Drink Coke!" The Vagrant cackled. And that was the second time this day the man was overcome with nausea.

"S'alright though," the Vagrant said calmly, and peered directly at the man. "It'll all be broke. Broke open wide for the truth and the truth's face."

"Who are you?" the man blurted out.

"Not about the who, brother." The Vagrant laughed and held out his right hand. "Call me Y. Spelled *Y*." He traced the letter in the air with his left hand and shook the man's hand with his right. Then his face changed. "Oh, Jake," he said, and this startled the man, for he'd certainly never informed the Vagrant of his name. The man tried to pull his hand away, but Y's grip was too strong. "Do you know where she is?" Y asked.

A train roared into the station.

"I can't find her," Y said, and began to cry.

"I'm sorry," the man stammered as he freed himself and ran to the train.

"I can't find her!" Y crumpled into sobs as the train doors closed behind the man. "I can't find my wife."

***

"Fucking idiots!" a driver screamed as they sped past the man and the woman standing in the middle of the bridge's vehicle lanes.

"Well, we're in a pickle," said the man.

"Time is tickell!" the woman responded. "Chaunce is fickell!"

"What?"

"Man is brickell! Freilties pickell!"

"What are you…"

"This is no pickle," the woman scoffed. "This is just a moment that necessitates decisive action."

"If we stay here, we can't jump."

"Then we better pick a side."

An SUV bore down on them, meandering erratically in and out of the eastbound lane.

"Someone's DUIing," said the woman.

"They're gonna hit us."

"We can let them."

"I've survived worse."

The SUV came closer. The woman grabbed the man's hand. "Back to plan A," she said, and led him away from the SUV to the pedestrian platform on the north side of the bridge, the side she'd chosen to begin with.

"Guess you win," said the man.

"We both win," she said, and dropped his hand and climbed over the rails to the unsafe side.

The man followed. "Can I ask you a—"

"No," she said, leaning against the rail and looking out at the city lights.

"I can't ask—"

"No."

"We're standing here about to… and I can't—?"

"Fine. Limit your questions."

"How many?"

"Three. No, I'm not your genie. You get two questions."

"I'm Jake by the way."

"Hi."

"And you—"

"Joy. You have one question left."

Jake shook his head. "Okay. How did you—"

"Don't," she cut him off again, "waste your question on asking me how I got here. That would take a whole novel to explain."

Jake looked out at the lights of the condos and office buildings and tower cranes settled on the left bank of the river below. "May I ask you then, Joy, why you chose this way?"

"You may not. Because you just used your second question."

Jake groaned in annoyance.

Joy shivered against the night breeze. "Opening my wrists would have been very messy."

"Not if you do it in the tub."

"For that, throw your hair dryer in the tub. Much cleaner."

"You could survive that."

"You could."

"I was gonna use my gun," Jake said. "I'd practice every morning."

"How do you practice that?"

"Hold it to your head unloaded and pull the trigger."

"Work up your nerve?"

"Train the muscle memory."

"Did your muscles keep forgetting?"

Jake leaned back, gripping the cold steel of the bridge's rail. "I felt bad for my landlord. I was like, if I do this, I'm gonna leave so much property damage for the guy."

The two shared a laugh. "So why this way?" Joy asked.

"I asked you first, and you never really answered," said Jake.

"Now I'm asking you," she said.

Jake followed the diminishing light of a plane flying high overhead. He looked like he wanted to speak but couldn't get the words out.

Joy smiled and carefully reached for his hand. "Yes," she said. "I wanted to feel like I was flying too."

Jake took her hand and looked into her eyes, the prettiest he'd ever seen in his life—warm brown with a barely discernible ring of blue. "We won't really be flying," he said, "just falling."

"Well, Jake," she said, and sadly smiled, "I guess we're two birds who don't fly so well."

Still holding hands, Jake and Joy faced the city lights and the river below. Jake's stomach grumbled. Joy squeezed his hand. "Ready?"

Jake pushed aside musings and reveries on the springtime romance he'd maybe share with this woman, this Joy, if he convinced her to climb back over the rails and go get a cup of coffee. But it wasn't going to get any better than this moment right here, right now. Besides, he never drank coffee. As for Joy, she thought of the taste of lemon-rosemary scones. Jake squeezed her hand back. "Ready."

Now… the equation is simple.

Velocity is equivalent to acceleration multiplied by time. In ideal, frictionless circumstances, the force of gravity would increase Jake and Joy's speed by approximately twenty-two miles per hour with each passing second. Of course, such ideal, frictionless circumstances never exist and as such, on the third second, due to wind resistance, Jake and Joy would have reached a speed somewhere around fifty-five miles per hour and Jake, still gripping Joy's hand, would have thought, "Maybe I shouldn't have done this..."

But then they hit the shattering cold.

***

... before I got one last slice of pizza. With extra cheese.

There wasn't darkness. Or light. There was just a splotchy red with barely perceptible lines of yellow. Jake felt his lungs expand. Contract. *A lemon-rosemary scone would have been great too. No, it wouldn't, I don't like scones. Actually, I don't know if I like them or not, I don't think I've ever had one. I'd eat anything right now, I'm starving. And now I'm in purgatory because of my grand sin and I'm going to be stuck here for Eternity thinking about pizza. And scones.* His lungs expanded again. *Maybe I'm not in purgatory, maybe I'm just in a coma. Ugh, that's even worse. Or not. Didn't someone once write a whole book while they were in a coma? I hear beeping. Maybe I'm in a hospital, I hope they feed me. I'm hungry. Throat's dry too. Could go for some H_2O. Got an itch behind my left ear. Does the view get any better besides all this red? Hold up. I think I can...*

Jake opened his eyes.

Now there was light. Too much light. It stung him in that area behind his temples. Jake yelped and shut his eyes, then reopened them slowly. Something was off. His body felt like it was encased in a plastic shopping bag. He sat up and leaned on his elbows, and in this manner awoke from uneasy thoughts to find himself in a bed, into *something* transformed.

What that something was, Jake was not sure. But whatever it was, at least he didn't feel like an unclean animal unsuitable for sacrifice. He felt very clean. Cleaner than he'd ever felt before, in fact. And he most certainly felt suitable for sacrifice.

Jake's eyes adjusted to the light. With some difficulty, he moved his head from side to side, taking in his surroundings. There was a wall-mounted patient monitoring system on the left side of his bed, but he wasn't attached to it. So, he was in a hospital, but he didn't seem to have undergone surgery. His feet felt weird. Like they were swollen. They were covered with a sheet that reeked of bleach and Jake threw off this sheet and saw his feet and blurted out, "The fuuuuuuuuuuuuuuuuck?"

He dropped his legs off the bed and stood, looking down at his body and doing his best to understand what was occurring. There was a full-length mirror by the door of the small, windowless hospital room. He nervously approached it.

Jake appraised his reflection, taking note of the spindly yellow legs and oversized feet with four toes. His white body. His feather-covered hands. His face was still his face, but he was shocked, yet also impressed, to see the large, red, protuberant comb that now adorned his brow.

Jake blinked and breathed and rationalized. He had heard of this before. Doctors who used humor and the healing power of laughter to treat their patients. This hospital probably just had some of those well-meaning, progressive, holistic, granola-eating, flakey-flake hippies prancing around with their newly minted Caribbean med school degrees. But still, Jake wondered as he unsuccessfully tried to find a zipper or a button or a piece of Velcro, would they really have gone so far as to put him in a full-body chicken suit?

"Jake!"

He cocked his head at the sound of his name screamed from somewhere beyond the room's door.

"Are you here?"

He opened the door.

Now there was information. Too much information. It stung him behind his temples. He shut his eyes, then reopened them, slowly.

"Jake, what is this!"

He looked at the world before him. It was hard to put into words. It reminded him of that day his mother had taken him to the Museum of Modern Art when he was nine—the day the riots started—and stood him before a black-and-white drawing by an artist named M.C. When Jake learned the artist's name, he did the Running Man and freestyled "Yo, I'm M.C. Escher and I'm here to say..." But then he couldn't come up with a next line. Also, his mother swatted his arm and told him to be serious, so he did and that's the end of that flashback.

"Jake!"

It wasn't funny this time, though. How everything looked. Because it wasn't in a drawing on a wall; it was real. Adrenaline pumped through Jake's veins, and he forced himself to count as he breathed in. One. Two. Three. Four. Hold. One. Two.

Three.

Four.

CHAPTER 2

There was a suburban corporate campus.

If one were to enter this campus by whatever means presently available, be they automotive or self-propelled, one would notice the bulky, rectangular, stainless-steel plaque embedded in a free-standing concrete foundation rooted in exquisitely maintained loamy soil furbished with lilyturf, mixed Grade-A polished garden stones, and Forest Green oak trees—the leaves of which were actually forest green at the moment, sunlight sneaking through their deciduous curves to glint off the steel plaque's stylized spelling of its redoubtable logo:

HG INC.

A pretty blue scrub jay landed on the plaque and screamed.

A cement-tiled walkway led past the scrub jay's screech to the center of the campus square, where there was a main building no more than three stories high (non-imposition!), fitted together with the precise interlocking of milled aluminum (industry!) and cold-bent laminated glass (transparency!). Inside this building, worker ants scurried between open-concept floor levels on symmetrically intersecting escalators, wide grins straining their cheeks, smartphones and warm lattes taxing their extensor carpi…

But one of those ants was in the know.

Her formfitting petite Luxe Suiting longline jacket—maroon with matching pants and pointy-toe pumps—was a blur, zipping with stylish efficiency through congregations embarking on intellectual collisions. She ran up the glass-paned escalators to the wood-paneled top floor and into an access-controlled point of ingress. She swiped her passive proximity access badge across the reader device attached to a door, and while waiting the quarter of a second for the 125-kilohertz communication between card and reader to transpire, tensed like an Olympic sprinter salivating at the starting blocks. The reader beeped. The door clicked. The race was on.

She burst into a hallway and ran to another door, her voluminous red hair trying its best to keep up. The door was cracked open; a sonorous tenor emitted from behind it:

"Have you ever proved your citizenship from an ATM? You will."

She entered the office and urgently stared at the long-haired, white-robed man who stood before a floor-to-ceiling window overlooking the corporate campus, his back facing her.

"Sir," she said, catching her breath.

"Have you ever kept an eye on the one you love from a distance legally mandated by that restraining order…"

"Sir…"

He lowered his voice to a whisper. "… or performed cunnilingus through your phone? You will."

"Mr. Gnosis," she said firmly, and the man clenched and unclenched his fists, then wiped his palms on his robe.

"Madelyne," he said, his back still facing her because if he turned to face her we would have to face the necessity of describing his face and that would prematurely reveal a major plot point. "I think we're on a first-name basis by now."

"You've been changing your name a lot more often, it's a little difficult to keep up."

"Oh, come on," Gnosis scoffed. "I've always kept it within the same themes, the same genres, the same motifs."

"The prophecy's happened," she said.

"Which prophecy?" he asked cautiously. "There's this, like, ridiculously overwhelming number of those lately. I want a new department. The Keep-Track-of-All-Prophecies Department. Note that. Do that. Get that started."

"The egg's been broken, sir."

Gnosis froze. Somewhere—not nearby, but somewhere—a thunder crack boomed.

"It's the Twin Chickens," Madelyne continued. "They've awoken. It's starting."

"And… how do you feel?"

"I feel fine. Don't you think—"

"No, I mean, how are *you*? How do *you* feel?"

Madelyne held back her exasperation. "We need to separate the Chickens. Now. Should I call in the Executive Board?"

"No, please, that's like, uber-overkill. How long have the Chickens been awake?"

"An hour? Maybe two? They're still in the hospital."

"Then they're still confused. Make sure they don't ever leave the hospital. Like ever, ever, in the history of ever. We don't want them finding you-know-who, what's he calling himself these days?"

"According to the Intel Unit," Madelyne said, "Sahib. Ponth J. Sahib."

"Ponth J…" Gnosis burst out laughing. "Ah, I see… If the *J* stands for… oh, that's… that's clever. That's adorably clever." Then his mood changed. "That fuck. Under no circumstances can we have the Chickens find him and his WVFF fucknut, fuckface… *Fucks!*"

Madelyne remained impassive.

"Which hospital are they in?" Gnosis asked.

"Saint Veronica's."

"That one of ours? Sounds like one of ours."

"We have that facility under complete control."

"Perfect. Call them up and alert the Misguidance Counselors."

"Already done."

"Look at you!" Gnosis said. "All on top of shit. Yeah! Now, as a contingency, let's think a few moves ahead…"

"That would be brilliant."

"Right? So let's also get the Miscommunication Unit on standby."

"Excuse me?" Madelyne said.

"The Miscommunication Unit. Call them. Put them on standby."

"So," Madelyne said, "what you're saying is you want me to—"

"Ugh," Gnosis muttered. "I forgot evoking the name of that unit alone causes problems."

"When you say, 'that unit,' you mean—"

"Just alert the Misguidance Counselors."

***

Too. Much. Information.

The first thing Jake noticed, as he struggled to get his heart rate down to a level that would permit him to make cognitively adequate decisions in an extraordinarily chaotic environment, were the stairs—winding to his left in true, endlessly circular Penrosian fashion—upon which at least a hundred, in Jake's estimation, of the hospital's denizens ceaselessly walked up and up and up without really going anywhere.

The second thing he noticed was the line. A countless number of people in various stages of pain and discomfort waiting in a snaking, seething, sinuous, lingering length of a line that extended into infinity. And at the front of this line was a woman who stood before a desk, behind which sat a man dressed in sky-blue medical scrubs, probably an intake nurse. And that was okay. That was somewhat familiar. Jake's mind could grasp that. It wasn't too sensually shocking, even as the woman screamed at the top of her lungs "*but my heart hurts!*" and the nurse shrugged his shoulders, passed her a clipboard, and pointed to the Penrose stairs.

"You're an idiot!" the woman screamed. "You're useless!" And that, too, was okay.

What was not okay were the flying monkeys.

Jake wasn't sure where they came from. The nurse screamed at the woman in a language Jake could not recognize. Russian? Czech? The woman screamed back in the same language, and suddenly there they were. They reminded Jake of the winged monkeys from the 1939 film version of *The Wizard of Oz*, but not really. They weren't clothed and blue with feathered wings. They were small and naked with wings more akin to those of bats, and they weren't entirely monkey either: Their brown heads and fur-covered torsos belonged to those of your average arboreal simian, but their lower bodies seemed to have been spliced from cherubic infants.

And part cherub or not, they were grotesquely violent. One landed on the shoulder of the woman, and the other landed on the head of the nurse. As the nurse and the woman screamed, the monkeys hooted and hollered and screeched, then flew at each other with teeth and claws and bit at each other's faces, drawing blood, and Jake had to close his eyes again, for this was absolute pandemonium in the truest, purest sense of the word as it was originally invented; that is, the place of all demons.

The place. Of all. Demons.

That needed some poignant, pregnant repetition. Just for fun. Just to elicit a moment of thematic reflection. If this were a movie, it'd be said with trombones going off in the background, yeah, with some souped-up post-production percussion and…

"Agh!" Jake screamed, and put his hands over where his ears should have been.

Let's dial down the percussion. Might have been too loud.

Jake turned to his right, disoriented from what sounded to him like a sudden burst of bass that just as quickly faded, and peered down a narrow hallway lit by flickering fluorescent tubes above. There was someone else at the end of said hallway, and this individual was also wearing a full-body chicken suit, albeit a suit whose fleshy red comb did not protrude as gallantly as his. This individual was struggling with three orderlies against a wall, and as she screamed "Jake, where are you?", Jake realized it was none other than Joy.

He jogged down the hallway, cautiously; he still didn't know what was going on.

"Haloperidol, let's go," one of the orderlies said in a voice that sounded muffled by a sock.

"Don't touch me!" Joy roared.

"Hey," Jake said upon approach. "Guys, what's the deal with—"

But he froze as the orderlies faced him. For they had no faces.

"This is sick!" Joy said. "A bad, sick joke and it's not funny!"

Jake tried to process why they appeared to have no faces. Masks? A trick of the lighting? But then he realized such rationalizations were pointless at the moment. What was clear and unequivocal was that the three faceless orderlies had just been joined by two more. And these additional Faceless Ones were holding syringes.

They went for Joy first. "No no no," Jake said, shoving them away and instinctively collecting her in his arms, turning himself into her protective meat shield. She buried her head under his chin. She smelled like candy and spring. Then he felt a pinch in his left deltoid and the world began to spin. "What'd you start with?" a muffled voice asked. "Forty-five," answered another. "Guy's about ninety kilos," said the first. "You want to OD him now?"

Jake looked down to meet the stable eyes of Joy in this spinning world. He tried to think of something positive to say as he met her gaze, expecting to encounter terror or tears. What he found, instead, as a Faceless One plunged a syringe into her shoulder, was laughter.

"I take it back," she said as their bodies slid down the wall to the floor. "This is kind of funny."

***

There was an ice cream truck.

The ice cream truck was a converted 1988 GMC P3500 step van bought on eBay by its current driver for approximately $8,500. It was painted white and pastel blue, and it played "Do Your Ears Hang Low" as it pulled its passenger side up to a sidewalk in the busy downtown district in the middle of the afternoon.

Two small children and their mother approached. The children, a boy and a girl, gaily enunciated their singing pitch in perfect chipmunkish tessitura: *"Do your ears hang low? Do they wobble to and fro? Can you tie 'em in a knot? Can you tie 'em in a bow?"*

"Are you shitting me right now!" a voice exploded from inside the truck.

The children froze. Their mother furrowed her brow and knocked her knuckles on the passenger side of the van. The driver, clutching his cell phone, appeared at the side window that was bedecked with pictures of popsicles, cones, and cookie sandwiches. The mother said angrily, "My kids would like—"

"You sure this ain't another false alarm?" the short, swarthy Ice Cream Man yelled into his phone.

"Excuse you!" the mother said.

"Chicken suits?" the Ice Cream Man continued into his phone. "Two of them? You positive... ? Which one... ? Saint Veroni... of course they took 'em there."

"Are you damaged?" the mother shouted.

"Ooookay." The man ignored her. "Tell Finance they gotta buy me another truck. One with a different song next time. Can't be responsible for corrupting the minds of minors."

He pocketed his phone and turned his attention to his customers. "You hear that?" he said to the children. "Stop singing that song, it's a dirty song."

"Suck my dick," the boy said as his sister flared her middle finger.

"See what I mean?" the man said to the mother.

"My children," the mother said, "would like..."

But the Ice Cream Man had already withdrawn from the window. The truck rocked on its wheels from the quickly shifting weight inside. Then it took off, tires screeching.

"Jackass!" the mother shouted after the truck as it quickly gained speed and ran straight into a lamppost.

***

"The purpose of this," the Psychiatrist said in a voice smoother than K-Y Jelly, "is to reduce certain, I don't want to say negative, but rather, *intervening* factors. Alienation. Withdrawal. The loss of self-esteem. So let's remember to listen. Let's remember to prepare this space and this time for each other. Okay?"

The four additional patients who sat in a circle with Jake and Joy nodded and muttered their affirmation. Joy giggled. Jake, next to her, squinted at the harsh lighting overwhelming the hospital room. The Psychiatrist, sitting at a point in the circle directly across from Jake and Joy, continued, "Wonderful. With that, let's welcome Jake, yes? And Joy. Would one of you like to start the conversation today?"

"Oh, yes," Joy said without hesitation, and clasped her

feathered hands in a gracious but regal manner. "Thank you, thank you. And hello." She gestured to the other patients. "Good tidings and good morrow and good dawning to you all."

Jake folded his arms and cocked an eyebrow beneath his fleshy red comb.

The Psychiatrist smiled. "Good tidings to you as well, Joy. How would you like to begin?"

She smiled back. "Why the fuck are we in these chicken suits?"

The Psychiatrist's teeth smiled but his eyes didn't. Jake noticed this and tensed, sitting straighter and planting both feet (with their new opposable toes) on the luxury vinyl tile flooring.

"I apologize," the Psychiatrist enunciated with caution. "I am at fault for having not laid out the, not so much the rules, but the *guidelines*. For effective facilitation of our—"

"No, no," Joy said, aping his manner of speech. "I am in fact the one who is, I don't want to say *required*, but rather, prompted, encouraged, *inspired*, to—"

"Clearly you have a formidable articulation at your command," the Psychiatrist talked over her. "Would it not be more beneficial to everyone if this command were utilized in place of obscenities, vulgarities, profanities..."

"And it is much appreciated," Joy said, "the avoidance of conflict in the usage of the passive voice. But I, you see, I..." And with this, she stood from her chair while Jake watched. "I demand to be an *active* character!"

Jake shifted in his seat. The other patients muttered incoherently.

"And this is a valid desire..." said the Psychiatrist.

"Demand," said Joy.

"... but the use of profane—"

"*My* usage," said Joy, "of the profane is *my* choice in making *my* point and *my* demand. And I want to know..."

"Joy..." Jake said as he noticed the Psychiatrist glance toward the opening double doors at the front of the room.

"... why," Joy continued, "the fuck, are we in these chicken suits?"

The Psychiatrist forced another smile. The other patients rubbed their forearms and stared at the floor in silence. Jake kept his eyes on the now-open double doors. A growling singing voice echoed into the room:

"Do your balls hang low? Do they dangle to and fro?"

Jake unfolded his feathered arms as a Faceless One entered. Joy turned toward the commotion, annoyed at the interruption. A second Faceless One followed the first, pushing a short, swarthy man in a wheelchair. The man continued to sing:

"Can you tie them in a knot? Can you tie them in a bow?"

The first faceless orderly approached the Psychiatrist and said in a low voice that Jake and Joy strained to hear, "Drove his ice cream truck into a lamppost on purpose."

The Psychiatrist nodded. "Stay by the door, please."

The orderly nodded in return, and the second Faceless One wheeled the Ice Cream Man into the circle. Then the two orderlies posted themselves by the double doors.

The Ice Cream Man stared directly at Jake and Joy and finished his song.

"Can you sling them on your shoulder like a lousy fucking soldier? Do your balls? Hang? Low?"

"Welcome, sir," the Psychiatrist said. "To start with, it would be most advantageous if—"

"Man, you can ass-wax poetic all you like," the Ice Cream Man said, not taking his eyes off Jake and Joy, "on Woolf, Conrad, Joyce, Eliot, Stein, Kafka. But the epitome of Modernism is in that song. Right there."

Jake narrowed his eyes. Joy cocked her head to the side.

"Humor and rage and deconstructed innocence," the Ice Cream Man continued, "chanted in the trenches of one of the most horrific events humanity's ever experienced. Passed on and on and on, and now it's a fucking ice cream truck melody. Like that First World War and all the wars that followed could be forgotten, and we could re-illusion the words and re-illusion ourselves and re-illusion our children to believe they don't live on a planet where they can get choked to death with weaponized chlorine or torn to shreds from IED shrapnel and two-twenty-threes hitting their little bodies at two thousand nine hundred and seventy…"

"Stop," Jake's voice cracked.

"… feet per second, while they're outside getting a chocolate/vanilla swirl on a waffle cone with rainbow fucking sprinkles."

Jake buried his head in his hands. Joy protectively put a hand on his shoulder.

"Sir," the Psychiatrist broke in, "let's please respect—"

"My question," Joy shouted. "Which has yet to be answered!"

"Let's start with that," the Psychiatrist said, trying to regain control. "No one here sees you wearing a chicken suit, Joy."

"Really?" Joy said to the group, and flapped her feathered arms. "No one else sees this?"

The four patients muttered and shook their heads no.

"That's what we were discussing," Joy said to the Ice Cream Man. "Before you rudely interrupted."

"Got it." The Ice Cream Man gave her a thumbs-up.

"Why do you believe you're wearing—" the Psychiatrist said.

"I have one on too," Jake said, touching the flesh of the red comb on his head.

The Ice Cream Man laughed to himself.

"I can see why you'd believe that, Jake," the Psychiatrist said, "given you both—"

"No," Jake said. "We didn't know each other before…"

"Then let's talk about what else you both see," the Psychiatrist said.

"Monkeys!" Joy said. "Crazy, little, mean, bat-baby-monkey monsters. Did you see those?" she asked Jake.

"Yeah," he said. "And the lines?"

"Forever," she responded.

"And the stairs?"

"Forever."

"Let's examine these shared delusions," the Psychiatrist said.

"Guys." The Ice Cream Man chuckled. "Don't listen to this

asshole. You're not deluded. You're disillusioned. And you have a shared worldview."

"Then you see the chicken suits?" Joy asked the Ice Cream Man.

The Ice Cream Man looked at Jake and Joy and smiled. For he, in fact, did not see a man and a woman in chicken suits. But what he did see forced a flood of emotion over his body. He chuckled and trembled and fought back tears. "It doesn't matter what I see, kid. If we're going to be successful, the two of you need to—"

"Who's 'we'?" Jake asked, his feathers bristling.

The Psychiatrist glanced at the two faceless orderlies and they approached the group. "What was your name again, sir?" the Psychiatrist asked the Ice Cream Man in the wheelchair, who now spoke to Jake and Joy in rapid fire. "Guys, you've awoken. This asshole's a Misguidance Counselor, he's trying to put you back to sleep."

The faceless orderlies rushed the Ice Cream Man from both sides, but he was small and quick, and he spun out of his wheelchair and jumped on one's back, gripping the Faceless One in a rear naked chokehold he refused to release as they both crashed to the floor. The other four patients threw their hands over their heads and ran out of the room. But the Psychiatrist simply turned his chair to face the fight and calmly folded his legs.

"Think about it!" the Ice Cream Man shouted, squeezing the orderly's neck and dodging the kicks of the second Faceless One. "I bet they shot you up with Haloperidol, right? Why are they hitting you with anti-psychotics the moment you wake? They never even talked to you!"

Joy, still standing, grabbed Jake's hand. Jake looked up at her from his chair.

"You're not crazy!" The Ice Cream Man struggled with the faceless orderlies on the floor. "You're awake! You see the truth! You've had a shift!"

Jake stood, holding Joy's hand, and peered into her eyes. "A perspective shift," he said.

Joy shook her head. "A *perception* shift."

Jake grunted. "Our point of view is different, right? It's a perspective shift."

"No." Joy stamped her four-toed feet. "We literally see things differently. It's a perception shift."

"Chickens!" the Ice Cream Man said, breathless from the effort of wrestling with the orderlies on the ground. "Get your shit together and come to an agreement on how you define your shared worldview! Because you're gonna have to work together on much crazier shit down the road."

Jake squeezed Joy's hand. "I'm only sure of two things right now," he said. "One. We need to get. Out. Of this hospital. Agreed?"

"Agreed."

"Two. We need to stick together. No matter what."

Joy looked into his face, a face cut rugged by what she could tell were dells dug by streams of distress, and somewhere there in that face, beneath the layers of all his years, she swore she saw, framed by the feathers and the beak and the comb, the countenance he'd likely conveyed frequently as a boy—open, candid. No agenda. No guile. He met her eyes, and she found it hard to breathe.

"No matter what?" she managed to croak.

"No matter what."

Then a light bulb appeared over their heads.

Literally.

It was a fifteen-watt clear glass bulb that materialized out of thin air and hovered over their heads, free and unattached. They both reached for it and grasped it and brought it down into their open palms. It lit up, and they giggled like children, and they said at the same time:

"*Perspection* Shift! We're having a Perspection Shift!"

"About time." The Ice Cream Man grunted and pushed away the orderly he'd rendered unconscious with his chokehold. But the second Faceless One leapt upon him, gripped the front of his throat, and squeezed. "Who are you?" the Faceless One screamed. The Ice Cream Man smashed his fist into the Faceless One's jaw, knocking him out.

"Sahib, motherfucker," the Ice Cream Man said, breathlessly

struggling to stand. "Ponth J. Sahib."

At that, the Psychiatrist sprung to his feet and rushed Ponth J. Sahib, only to be intercepted by a quickly moving Jake, who dispatched him with a feathered elbow to the head.

"Wow," Joy said. "Couldn't do that before?"

Jake ignored the gibe and pulled Ponth to his feet. They faced the double doors. The echoes of scores of running feet reverberated into the room.

"They're coming," Joy said. "All the Faceless Ones."

"We're gonna have to fight our way out of here," said Ponth. "You guys ready?"

"No," said Joy.

"No one's ever ready," said Jake.

The stampede outside the double doors grew louder. Joy grabbed a chair. Jake raised his clenched fists.

"Well, Chickens," Ponth said, and cracked his neck and smiled, "let the revolution begin."

CHAPTER 3

There was a bar.

Actually, it wasn't a bar, it was a restaurant. But the restaurant had a bar, and sitting at the counter of the bar that made us, in a synecdochical manner, call the restaurant the bar—even though the bar was just a small section in the rear of the restaurant—was a woman who cried *"fucking asshole!"* and slammed her palm against the ash-wood countertop of the bar.

She ignored the startled, nugatory glances of the bar's current denizens, and the bartender, a hulk of a man, sauntered over. "Refill on the porter?" he asked. The woman waved her hand. "Let me try that IPA." The bartender grabbed her mug, ran it under a tap, then returned it.

"Everything I tolerated," the woman continued. "All those many, many, I don't even know. *Years* isn't the right word. All that *time*. Time filled with 'You want to move, honey? Okay, I'll follow you.' 'Honey, is that really a good way to raise our son? Okay, I'll trust you.'" She took a swig of her pale ale. "The other women?" she slurred. "Tolerated… all of them."

"Now," said the bartender. "He really say he ain't coming back? Or is that a creative addition on your part?"

The woman took another swig. "He said what he always says. That he has to follow…" She wiggled her fingers in the air. "The Calling."

"I could…" the bartender said.

"Fuck his calling."

"I could find him."

"I think he's jealous," she said.

"Of?"

"The kids are out. I went back to work, and I-I *love* my job. It's exciting and engaging and it's, it's important. I'm the one who's involved now. I'm in the mix. I'm the important one."

"Which is who he's used to being."

"I think he made it all up. He couldn't handle me working,

and he left. He left."

"I could find him, and, you know."

The woman laughed. A long, hoarse laugh carrying the subharmonic spectra of all the laughter from all her years. "Oh, my little Nimrod," she said. "Because that worked so well for you the first time."

The bartender sheepishly chuckled. "That's cold."

"Couldn't help it."

"You know how fucked up it feels when your name's a dis?"

"Blame Bugs Bunny."

"It was Daffy Duck."

"It was Bugs."

Nimrod the bartender shook his head. "That's how everyone remembers it, 'cause they racist."

"Against ducks?"

"Daffy was Black. Watch them shits. Daffy always getting played while the white rabbit gets to be the player."

"Bugs was a little gray."

"He had that drop in him, you know, from his great-granddaddy Br'er. But dude was passing. Daffy was unambiguously Black. And Daffy goes and says a joke that changes the world, and everyone gives the credit to Bugs."

"The important point," the woman said with a smirk, "is you're not mad about my joke."

"The important point is Daffy was a brother. That gives the joke a subtle complexity I can appreciate."

The woman laughed again.

"Don't laugh," Nimrod said. "That's the funny thing about jokes. They always point to some serious shit. What you need to be thinking on, is how bad it's gotten out here that everyone, you included, thinks the joke started with Bugs." He set his face, stoic. "That's how far-reaching our enemy has become."

The woman quietly lifted her mug. "Buzzkill," she grumbled. But before she could drink, her smartphone rang. She put down her mug and pulled her phone out of her purse and squinted at the caller ID. "Interesting timing," she said to Nimrod, then answered the call. "This is Sarah... Hey, Ponth... nope, just with Nimrod... wait, slow down... what in... Where are you?"

***

"Saint Veronica's," Ponth said into his cell. "Use that find-my-phone shit and get eyes on me... Thank you, Sarah." He ended the call.

"You got a date or something?" Jake said with his fists clenched and raised as the first of the Faceless Ones rushed into the room.

"Look at you, all bold," Ponth said, not taking his eyes off the second, third, fourth, and fifth of the Faceless Ones who entered and spread out. "'Bout to get into the brawl of our lives and you're cracking jokes like a Ninja Turtle."

"Don't change the subject, mysterious Ice Cream Man. Who's Sarah, your side piece?"

"If you only knew all the poor souls who tried to make her their side piece."

Joy raised the chair she'd grabbed over her head.

"I'm not hitting anyone with this chair," she said.

Joy raised the chair she'd grabbed over her head.

"No," she said. "I'm not hitting anyone with this chair."

"You okay?" Jake asked her, fighting back a newly creeping sense of nausea.

"I can see it," Joy muttered.

The Faceless Ones closed in.

"I can see it!" Joy disploded. "I can see *both*!"

She dropped the chair and ran over to Ponth. "You. Ice Cream Man."

"Sahib. Ponth J—"

"Ponth J. Ice Cream Man. You need to leave."

"Ponth J. Sahib doesn't run from a fight," he said. A flying bat-monkey-cherub thing appeared, squatted on top of his head and screeched.

"Whoa!" Jake said, recoiling. But Joy swung and backhanded the flying monkey off Ponth's head. It careened into a wall and vanished with a *poof*. Ponth clutched his chest.

"Oof," he said. "You're right. Let my ego get in the way there. What's your plan?"

"Guys," a Faceless One said, "let's keep things copasetic."

Ponth, Jake, and Joy huddled. "Ponth," Joy said, "if you have people on the outside, you need to get to them in case what happens with me and Jake doesn't work."

"I can't get out of here, kid, there's no windows or—"

"There's a window right there." Joy pointed to the wall behind them.

"How'd I miss that?" Ponth said.

"We all did," said Joy. "Someone didn't put it in the description."

"The description of what?" asked Jake.

"There's no time!" said Joy, flustered as the Faceless Ones closed in. "Ponth, please trust me. Go!"

"Fine," grumbled Ponth. Then he sprinted and leapt headfirst out the small open window.

"Damn it," a Faceless One said, and two of his cohorts ran out of the room.

"I can't fit through that," Jake said, glancing at the window. "You can, though."

"No," Joy said, grasping his hand. "We stick together. No matter what. Right?"

"Yeah, but—"

Joy tugged on his arm and forced him to lean down to her height. She brought her mouth to his ear and whispered. The remaining three Faceless Ones approached, pulling out zip-tie cuffs.

"That's crazy," Jake said to her, standing up straight.

"Trust me." Joy smiled. "I can see both."

"Okay," Jake said. Then the three Faceless Ones charged.

Joy sat in the chair, folded her arms, and watched Jake spring into action. The man was a doctoral-level study in the effective application of focused violence. The three Faceless Ones rushed

Jake sat in the chair, folded his arms, and watched Joy spring into action. The woman was only about five feet tall, but she seemed to grow in stature as she threw back her shoulders and sharply strode to meet him, overconfident in their numerical advantage. The lead Faceless One stupidly held his zip-tie cuffs above his head as if he were trying to appear larger to a wild animal with a chase instinct. Jake was no wild animal. But he did have a chase instinct. He salivated and threw a right, smashing his curled fist into the Faceless One's open solar plexus. The Faceless One doubled over in agony, trying to catch his breath, and Jake uppercut him in the chin, knocking him to the floor, unconscious, while the remaining two combatants grabbed Jake by his neck and left arm. They dragged him to the ground and straddled him, doing their best to force his wrists into a pair of cuffs. Unfortunately, one brought himself a little too close to Jake's teeth, which Jake sank into the area where a cheek should have been. The Faceless One screamed and bled while Jake roared and managed to get his feathered hands on the screaming one's neck, gripping with all his might at the Faceless One's carotid arteries. The Faceless One struggled to get loose while his compatriot stood and kicked Jake in the chest and ribs. Jake took the toward the three Faceless Ones. The lead held up his zip-tie cuffs and haughtily said, "Let's be good, and these will be off you in no time."

"Get your clients' rights officer," said Joy.

The lead Faceless One stammered. "The… the rights—"

"The right one, yes. The wrong one won't help us, right? And that would be a violation of our…"

"Right," the Faceless One said, deflated.

"Exactly," Joy chirped.

Jake shook his head in admiration, then nearly fell out of his seat as a suit-wearing clients' rights officer appeared out of nowhere with a loud *poof*.

"I assume you want to leave," said the officer.

"And that has made an ass of neither you nor me," said Joy.

"You can't just leave."

"Then show us the county court order that says we can't just leave."

"We… the order…"

"Do you have one to keep us here?"

"We're going to have to press charges."

kicks, then positioned the combatant he held to act as a shield against the other's blows.

Joy tapped her four-toed foot impatiently. "How long is this going to take?"

"Seriously?" Jake panted and tried to control his breathing and wished he hadn't let himself get so out of shape.

"Hurry up," Joy said. "Before more come."

"I can't rush it," Jake gasped. "He'll pass out when he passes out."

The Faceless One in Jake's grip went limp while the other continued to rain kicks on Jake's torso. Jake released the newly unconscious Faceless One and grabbed the boot of the other, making him stumble as only one foot was on the ground. Jake kicked this foot out from under the last Faceless One, then leapt on top of him as he crashed to the vinyl floor. The Faceless One shouted for help and covered his face that wasn't actually a face with his arms, but Jake's punches got through anyway, their force doubled by the fact that every blow resulted in the back of the Faceless One's

"For what?" asked Joy.

"For that." The officer pointed to the laid-out Psychiatrist and the two Faceless Ones rendered unconscious in the last chapter.

"Then you'll have to press charges against the little Ice Cream Man who jumped out the window. Because that is who is responsible for that. And we are going to leave. Because *we* are not presently charged for any crime, and *you* don't have a court order to keep us here."

"Then you are going to have to submit a three-day letter to the medical director."

"And you are going to have to stop putting a modal verb on top of the future indicative. It's hurting my ears."

"Once your request to leave is submitted, the hospital will have three days to either let you go or file an affidavit with the court to keep you here. And I can tell you now, we will file that affidavit, and we will get that order."

"You didn't make an ass out of you and me, so don't make a *pres* out of you and head hitting the ground.

"Don't kill him!" Joy shouted.

"Eh," Jake said. "He'll be fine. This luxury vinyl flooring's pretty soft."

"It is soft," said Joy.

"Amazing how we noticed that but not the window that gave us a potential escape."

"Right?" said Joy.

The last Faceless One moaned, the fight beaten out of him. Jake staggered to his feet and hunched over, struggling to catch his breath. Joy got up and patted him on the back and walked past him toward the double doors. "Good job," she said, then paused at the exit. "You coming? Ing? Ing?"

me either—"

"Posterior Reversible Encephalopathy Syndrome may be exactly what you're—"

"Because for what you're saying about this three-day letter to make sense, you have to *presume* we are voluntary patients. I didn't volunteer to be here. Did you, Jake?"

"Nope," said Jake.

"And we're not involuntary, because you don't have an order that says so."

The clients' rights officer looked at the three Faceless Ones. "She's right, guys."

"Awwww," said the Faceless Ones.

"And now," said Joy, "I am shifting to the present progressive and we, are, leaving!" She walked to the door, then paused and turned to Jake. "You coming? Ing? Ing?"

Jake hustled toward Joy. "I guess I'm going to have to do that."

***

Madelyne burst into the executive office for the second time that day. "Mr. Gnosis!"

Gnosis, standing before his floor-to-ceiling window, his back still facing her, replied, "What have I said?"

"About what?"

"The name basis we are on?"

"We don't have time for—"

"As in, *first*?"

"The Twin—"

"Not second. Not third."

"Sir, the Twin Chickens have—"

"Lalalalalala…" Gnosis put his palms over his ears.

"You want to be informal," Madelyne muttered. "Yet you act like a pissant, always standing with your back to me."

"I do act puissant when I stand with my back to you. Even on a first-name basis, we have to maintain some decorum."

"That's not what I… I thought you weren't listening?"

"Lalalalalala…"

"Hip…" Madelyne said with a roll of her eyes.

"Yes? Madelyne? See? Was that so hard? Now we can talk, we can rap, we can communicate."

"Okay. Hip?"

"Yes?"

"The Twin Chickens have escaped."

Hip Gnosis put his forehead to the window.

"Fuuuuuuuuuuu…"

"What are your orders?"

"Hey, you can't just be all 'what are your orders.' I'm a little shook. I need, I need…"

"What do you need?"

"I need the 4-1-1, sheeeeeit. *W-T-F* went down?"

"Depends on the worldview."

"Start with the basic."

"Basic worldview? The female trounced our people with legal discourse. Smacked them around with some wordplay just for fun, then walked herself and the male right out."

"Dare I ask what happened from a disillusioned perspective?"

"I'd say it's from a disillusioned perception."

"Tomato, tomahto." Hip Gnosis groaned. "What happened?"

"The male beat everyone unconscious, then walked himself and the female right out."

"That means…"

"Yup," said Madelyne.

"They've already figured out how to act symmetrically."

"Yup."

"Which means, they can perceive..."

"See? It's a perception."

"... two worldview *perspectives* simultaneously."

"Well, the female can."

"The female?"

"The orderlies reported that before the Chickens launched their offense, the female told the male she could quote, see both, end quote."

Hip Gnosis leaned against the window again. "Any other pertinent details?"

"Ponth J. Sahib was there. He escaped too."

"Fuuuuuuuuu..."

"What are your orders, Hip?"

Hip Gnosis clenched a fist and forced himself not to smash it through the window. "Motherfucking, fucker, fuck..."

Madelyne waited. Hip Gnosis continued, "Little fucking, fuckety, fucker..."

"Two orderlies have eyes on Ponth," Madelyne said. "They've been keeping me apprised."

"Ponth hasn't surfaced since..."

"The '30s."

"It's been longer than that."

"The 1830s," Madelyne clarified.

Hip Gnosis ran a hand through his shoulder-length hair. "Now, why did we just feel the need to say out loud things we already know?"

"Not sure. But I'd like to think we said them subtly and within the natural context of our conversation."

"No doubt. We don't want to get all expositional."

"Can't have that," said Madelyne. Then Hip Gnosis's head burst into flames.

The room's temperature rose quickly, and Madelyne had to step back toward the door. The color of fire shifts from the red end to the blue-violet end of the visible light spectrum as its temperature increases from 1,112 degrees Fahrenheit to anything beyond 2,552 degrees. Hip Gnosis's head flames were blue. A bead of sweat rolled down Madelyne's... not exactly her… This may be a good place to mention she, too, did not have a face…

"So dramatic," she muttered.

"MADELYNE," Hip Gnosis said in a voice seeming to emit from LCR speakers with the bass turned up after having been digitally reverberated with a long pre-delay so his words remained clear. "DO NOT FAIL ME. PLEASE. PRETTY PLEASE. WITH A MARASCHINO CHERRY ON TOP. ORDER THE ORDERLIES… THAT DOESN'T SOUND RIGHT. IT'S LIKE SAYING COMMAND THE COMMANDERS…"

"It's getting hot in here," Madelyne said impatiently.

"AND I HAVE SUCH A GOOD POP-CULTURE REFERENCE IN RESPONSE TO THAT," Hip Gnosis boomed, his voice shaking the floor-to-ceiling windowpane. "BUT IF I SAID IT OUT LOUD, IT WOULD CONSTITUTE WORKPLACE SEXUAL HARASSMENT AND I KNOW, I MEAN, EVEN THOUGH, I…" He reverted to his normal voice. "I want you to feel safe in…"

"The orderlies will continue to follow Sahib from a safe distance."

"Keep me updated," said Hip Gnosis.

"I will."

"If we're lucky, Sahib will lead us back to the WVFF."

"That would be… fortuitous," Madelyne said, then rushed out of the room.

"Yes! Fortuitous!" Gnosis called out after her. "Get on that, girl! I mean, woman! Because, I-I wouldn't… I mean, I didn't… you know, mean to disrespect you by…"

He trailed off and stared out the window. Then he hummed and danced alone to the copyright-protected song he'd referenced before.

***

Jake and Joy ran along the downtown waterfront as best they could with their new feet, or shoes covering their feet—they couldn't tell—that had three toes pointing forward and one pointing back.

"Can we stop now?" Joy said between breaths. "No one's following us."

Jake complied and... No. No. No. The story needs to maintain momentum with an effective passage of time here...

Let's fast-forward a bit:

JakecompliedandsaidwheredoyouliveIcanorderyouaridewithmyrideapponmyFitbitandJoyavoidedeyecontactandsaidIthoughtwewerestayingtogethernomatterwhatandJakesaidwecangotomyplaceIjustdidn'tknowifyou'dbecomfortablecomingtomyplaceandJoysaidlet'sgoandJakesaidlet'stakethesubwayandJoygotconfusedandsaidthesubway?andJakesaidyeahthere'ssomeoneinthesubwayIwanttoseeandJoysaidokaysotheywalkedtothesubwaysnuckpastaturnstilebecausetheyhadnomoneyorcardsorcellphonesonthemIguessyouleavethosethingsbehindwhenyou'replanningtocommitsuicidethentheywaitedonaplatformforaboutfifteenminutesthengotonatrainwhenitarrived.

The train roared through the tunnels and when its horn demonically blared, Jake thought of a basilisk cutting a swath through the fields of Tartarus. He and Joy huddled together in the corner seating of a car, trying to not make eye contact with the other commuters. For to do so was unnerving; most, not all, but most, were displaying black-and-white spirals in their eyes.

"Do you see that?" Jake muttered, and Joy nodded in confirmation.

"There could be an explanation," Joy ventured. "A reasonable explanation."

"Like?"

"Everyone's wearing spiral contact lenses? Like a Zombie Walk. Or the Naked Bike Ride!"

"I don't remember there being a citywide Let's-pretend-we're-in-a-cartoon-and-hypnotized Day."

"Let's ask," Joy said, and tilted her head toward the commuter in the seat across.

"Don't ask," said Jake.

"Relax." Joy patted his feathered knee. "I'll be subtle."

"Please be subtle."

"I'll be smooth."

"Please be smooth."

"*Hi there!*" Joy shouted at the commuter, startling him. "I like your contacts! Is today a special day?"

Jake tried to appear smaller. The commuter smiled uncomfortably. "My contacts?"

"Yes, your—" Joy pointed to her eye. "They're cool. Why is everyone wearing them?"

"I don't, I'm not… wearing contacts."

"Ohhh, okay, okay, okay," she said, and winked. Then she jumped to her feet and did a jumping jack. "Do you like my chicken suit?"

The commuter stood and rushed to the opposite side of the car. Joy cackled. Jake stared at her, incredulous.

"Don't look at me like that," she said.

"Like what?"

"With all your incredulity."

"My incre… I didn't say nothing."

"Yes, you did. I hear everything you say and don't say."

"What are you talking about?"

"Like before. When you thought the train was…" She lowered her voice and spoke as if she were narrating a movie trailer from the '90s. "… a basilisk. Cutting a swath through the fields of Tartarus."

Jake froze and the feathers on the back of his neck stood up. But Joy laughed so hard she had trouble getting her words out. "Where'd you even get language like that? If this were a novel, an editor would rightly ask, are there even fields in Tartarus? You read a lot of comic books, don't you? That's okay. I love comic books too. I love everything! Everything! But everything with you, Sir Jake, is just so darkly poetic, no?"

Jake sat silent, agape.

"But you know what a basilisk is to me?" Joy asked, and held her palms out about two feet apart. "It's just a lizard. About that big. From where I'm from. And we don't call him el basilisco. We call him el lagarto de jesucristo."

The train slowed. "Why do you call him that?" Jake asked.

Joy smiled. "Because he can run on water."

The train stopped. Jake grunted and shook off the shivers

running down his spine and stood. "Think I saw that shit on National Geographic."

Joy threw her shoulders back and did her best to growl. "Think I saw that shit on National Geographic. Think I'll ruin this profound moment with my tough-guy shit. Shit, shit, shit."

The doors opened with an electronic ring. The commuters shuffled and congealed. Joy wrapped an arm in Jake's, and they blended in with the madding crowd. "You need to loosen up," she said. "If we're going to be insane, we might as well have fun with it."

They stepped off the train. Then Joy let Jake go and poked her head back into the car before the doors closed. "*You're all fucking hypnotized!*" she screamed. Then she skipped down the subway platform like a little girl. Jake shook his head and jogged to catch up.

When he caught up, she slowed and put her arm back in his, and they made their way up a staircase, then down a tunnel whose walls and columns were saturated with video ads mounted at odd oblique angles over the ancient ceramic tiles. The ads broadcast deodorant and dating apps and divorce lawyers, and Jake tuned out their digital entreaties until he heard a voice.

"You've got to stop!" the voice echoed down the tunnel. "The answers are there. Written in your heart. Closer than your jugular!"

Jake picked up his pace, and now it was Joy's turn to keep up. "Why the rush?" she asked. They turned a corner and came upon the Vagrant, who sat camped at the base of a stairwell that led to an exit.

"That's why," Jake said.

"What's why?" Joy asked.

"No, who."

"What?"

"Who."

"Who's why?"

"He is."

"Where?"

"There," Jake said, pointing at the smiling Vagrant.

"I'm Y," the Vagrant gently addressed Joy. "Spelled *Y*."

"Ohhhh," Joy said, and giggled, and Y giggled with her. "I'm so sorry," she said. "I see you now." She squatted by Y and clasped both his hands in hers. "I'm Joy."

Y beamed at her. "That's what brother John said too."

"Who's John?" Joy asked.

"I will see you again," Y whispered, and peered at Jake. "You will rejoice. And no one will take away your Joy."

"Y," Jake said, and crouched beside him, "can you see our chicken suits?"

Y laughed and took his hands out of Joy's and appeared to fight back tears.

"You know what's going on, don't you?" Jake said. "You know about the monkeys and the Faceless Ones and the lines and the—"

"You know?" Joy asked. "You do? You know?"

Y nodded. "I know everything."

"Tell us!" Joy said.

"Y, tell us," Jake said. "Please."

"Tell you what?"

"Everything," said Jake.

"That's a lot to tell. Where would I even start?"

Jake and Joy looked at each other, then said at the same time, "The beginning."

Y laughed. "You sure?"

Jake and Joy nodded like children about to get a chocolate/vanilla swirl on a waffle cone.

"With rainbow sprinkles," said Joy.

"You are sure, with rainbow sprinkles," Y said, and shook his head and scratched his scraggly beard. "Well, alright. I'll start in the beginning."

Jake and Joy leaned forward.

"There was a big tent," Y said.

"What kind of tent?" asked Joy.

"Lamb hair," Y answered. "A lamb-hair tent in the vast desert, and once in a while, a rainbow sprinkle would pop up."

"Where?" said Joy.

"On the tent," said Y. "So the lamb hair would shift."

"For the sprinkle," said Joy.

"Exactly."

"Come on." Jake grunted and stood. "You're not making any sense."

Y, hurt by Jake's careless words, stopped talking and looked dejectedly at the ground.

Joy glared at Jake, then grabbed Y's hands again. "No, no, no. I'm sorry, don't pay attention to him. He's like, I don't know, everything you say is beautiful, he's just like… Eeyore! That's who I'm thinking of!"

"I'm not like—" Jake said.

"Yeah! Eeyore!" Joy said, and shot him another angry glance.

Y perked up and added vigorously, "That's what both of you are like. That's what you are."

"I'm not like Eeyore." Joy giggled. "Am I?"

Y giggled back. "Yeah, Eeyore. And here's the question."

"What's the question?" Joy leaned forward.

"Did the words make the lamb hair shift?" Y said. "Or did the shift make the words?"

"The shift…" Jake repeated, and narrowed his eyes.

"Ah," Y said, and winked at Joy. "Now the brother's thinking. It's the same question always. What came first? The chicken? Or the egg?"

Joy looked up at Jake. A silence hung between them. Then Joy said, "Don't do it."

"Don't do what?" said Jake.

"Don't ruin this profound moment."

"I don't understand this moment."

"Neither do I, but that doesn't matter."

"It will all break open wide," Y chimed in. "For the truth and the truth's face. Just be patient. Now you have to go." He pointed to the stairwell leading to the exit. "Go."

Joy stood and looked into Jake's eyes. They both fought back a creeping queasiness and struggled to breathe.

"No matter what?" Jake said, and held out his hand.

Joy averted her eyes and squinched her face. "You have to stop being a jerk."

"I'm not trying to be—"

"I know you have a lot of pain. I can feel it. But you have to stop."

"You have a lot of pain too."

"I know. We'll talk about everything. Eventually. But, I don't know, *try* to have fun."

"I'll try."

Joy put her hands behind her back and balanced on her tiptoes. "And don't hurt me."

Jake froze. "I would… I could never…"

"Promise," she said.

"I promise."

Joy let out a deep breath and put her hand in his. "Okay."

"Okay?"

"Okay."

"Okay," he said. "I still don't know what's going on."

"That's okay." She smiled.

They walked up the stairs, and Y watched them ascend and he fought back his giggles and his tears. They left the station, and Y wiped his eyes with his palms and scratched his beard and whispered, "Please find her. I know you two can do it. Please find my wife."

CHAPTER 4

There was a… Okay, this is the last time we'll do the "there was a" schtick…

There was a girl.

The details pertaining to this girl *do* matter—any random, subjective construct will actually not suffice. The girl's name was Edoma Berkley. Edoma was nineteen years old. This made Edoma technically a woman, but culturally, she was still very much a girl. Now, *personally*, that is, within the realm of Edoma's subjective agency and self-definition, she was—well, she wasn't really sure. There were too many things at that point in time Edoma was unsure of. Too many things she had once viewed with certitude that had only recently been upended, undone, and overturned. In regard to these things, Edoma was hoping her current task would lead to some form of closure, epiphany, or spiritual resolution.

She parked her car, a used silver Prius she had purchased a week prior, whose odometer now read: 102,374. She walked north on a parkway called Naito, a gleaming condominium complex to her right, a length of train tracks across the street to her left. She noticed a building with a water tower up ahead and it reminded her of home; you didn't see too many water towers out here. A Union Pacific locomotive clanged on the tracks across the street, pulling what had to have been a mile-long load of railcars. Cross traffic stopped and patiently waited for the industrial serpent to pass. Edoma double-checked the directions to an address in the maps app of her smartphone and made a right onto a pedestrian path that led her east toward the river. Behind her, the locomotive let loose a long, low howl.

The sun was setting as Edoma approached a guardrail overlooking the river. Across the river, on the opposite shore, a grain elevator rose against the cobalt sky like a titan of primordial old, while another behemoth, a cargo ship, pulled away from the elevator, floating lazily north. Edoma, for her part, made another right, turned south, and continued down the path, the river now to her left, the rear of the gleaming condominium complex she had circled around on her right.

She continued south, past ducks, benches, landscaped shrubs, and lovers going for evening strolls in the spring. This neighborhood was a definite step up from the previous three she had visited. Ahead, a reddish-orange bridge spanned over the river. Because of the interest sparked by that Introduction to Engineering and Design course she had completed last semester, before she'd dropped out, Edoma knew this bridge consisted of a truss design with a double-leaf, Rall-type bascule lift span. A twinge in her belly informed her she was on the right path.

The concrete pedestrian passage transitioned to the wooden planks of a boardwalk, and a different, topographically lower and older, condominium complex now lay on Edoma's right. She checked her phone once more, scanned the numbers on the condo apartments before her and, spotting the one she sought on the door of a ground-level unit, made her way down a walkway. She knocked.

Edoma waited and tugged at the bottom of her plaid button-down shirt. The shirt, like her hair, was dark red and slightly frizzy. Her complexion was pinkish and freckled. At nineteen, her body was still in that envy-inducing stage where it was somehow both thin and full, and Edoma was aware of this. She was, in fact, grateful for it given her current endeavor. People would generally be more receptive to the presence and inquiries of a stranger who was a reasonably attractive, if slightly tomboyish, red-headed white girl, than say, a stranger who was unattractive, too attractive, male, non-white, or any combination of the above. She crinkled her nose at the smell of the river behind her—decaying algae and gull poop. Then she knocked again.

A brunette white woman in her thirties answered the door. Edoma felt slightly relieved. The last home she'd visited, a bungalow in a trashy area east of the city proper, had been occupied by a man almost old enough to be her father, who'd, a little too readily, invited her in to share his couch and his weed. He was a creepy weirdo. Without stepping foot into the bungalow, however, she did convince him to give her a dimebag for free. It was good. Hydroponically grown. Way better than East Coast grass.

"You need something, hon?" the brunette said.

"Yes, sorry. I'm looking, for this guy…"

"Uh oh."

"No, it's not like that." Edoma blushed, turning redder than she already was. "He might live here. Or have lived here."

"You got a name?"

Edoma nodded and her throat went dry. "Yakov."

"Ya-who?"

"Yakov. Yakov Rabinowitz-Brown."

"Nuh uh. Definitely not."

Edoma looked at her phone, then at the number on the apartment door. "You sure?"

"What's he look like?"

"He's…" Edoma faltered.

"Tall, short? Black, white?"

"He's…" Edoma shrugged helplessly.

The woman stepped back into her apartment. "Sorry, hon. You have a good evening. Gorgeous outside."

"You too," Edoma muttered, and headed back the way she came.

The wooden boardwalk transitioned to the concrete walkway, and Edoma found and sat on a bench before the guardrail overlooking the river. She fought back tears. She was out of leads. The man she sought had no presence on Facebook, Twitter, LinkedIn, or Instagram, and after scouring sites like mylife.com, intelius.com, whitepages.com, clustrmaps.com, and even gongju5.com, Edoma had managed to cull one now-non-working cell phone number and four residential addresses affiliated with the target of her efforts. This address by the river was the fourth, and last, she had visited over the past four days. The response of each occupant was essentially no different than that of the woman with whom Edoma had just spoken.

She pulled out her smartphone. Perhaps she had overlooked an address, a phone number, something. She tapped and swiped at the screen, reading through the search results for Yakov Rabinowitz-Brown. Nope. Nothing new. Her heart sank. She felt lost. Lost and lonely and dejected. But mostly, she just felt stupid. She stood and consoled herself with the thought that waiting for her back in her new apartment was a little weed left over from the dimebag the creepy weirdo had given her the day before. Hopefully, her new roommate hadn't taken it. She moved to pocket her phone, but a targeted ad caught her eye. She tapped it. Her screen lit up with the image of a grinning, bald monk in red-and-yellow robes. She smiled. She loved this monk. And according to the ad, he was the keynote speaker at a Spiritually Uplifting Communal and Destiny Intensifying Conference to be held at the waterfront park named after a former, now-dead, state governor—located just a bit south of where she was at the moment—in a mere three days.

Edoma gazed again at the reddish-orange bridge. Perhaps she was meant to go to that conference. Perhaps that was why she felt that twinge in her belly every time she looked south down the river toward that bridge. Perhaps the universe really was conspiring in her favor, and she would find the resolution she sought in three days. And she wouldn't have to feel so lost, so lonely, and so stupid for having turned her back on everything and everyone back home to move to this far-flung town pretending to be a city in the farthest reaches of her country's Pacific Northwest. Yes. She was meant to be here. She was meant to listen to the monk, live and in person. She was meant. She had meaning.

Edoma Berkley smiled to herself and walked back to her car. In the distance, the receding train howled once more.

***

Joy's nerves fired and jerked her body awake, and she smashed her foot into a wall.

It's a surprisingly prevalent phenomenon, the hypnagogic jerk that is, and an evolution-based theory surmising its mysterious origin asserts, or rather accuses—for surmise comes to us from the Old French past participle of surmettre, to accuse—our primate ancestors to be the begetters (or to have gotten the begetting?) of a physiological reaction to an over-relaxation of muscles during sleep, as said over-relaxation would catastrophically result in our ancestors falling from the trees in which they slept and plummeting to their death, or to their serious physical injury, which in the riparian forests of the Messinian stage of the Miocene epoch was pretty much equivalent to death, hence the development of a spasmic reaction to the sense one gets that they're about to fall while asleep; a sense that kept our ancestors safe and sound, and allowed us to be here now, ruminating on etymology, geological epochs, and how best to end unnecessarily long and stupidly complex sentences.

The pain of Joy's stubbed toe trickled from calf to hamstring to buttocks to spinal cord and back down again, making her curl into a fetal position while she grabbed her foot. She did not blame her primate ancestors for her hypnagogic jerk. She blamed her memories. Besides, she wasn't sure she still was a primate. She held her foot, gripping the rubbery, yellow covering with three front toes and one rear, and realized she couldn't tell if the pain was coming from a digit underneath said rubbery covering or from a digit on the covering itself.

Her vision cleared. She was alone, in a tiny bedroom with a ceiling so low she knew if she sat up she could raise her arms and touch it. The bed she lay in appeared at first to be a king-size, but that was not the case. When she got out of the bed, she saw it comprised two twin mattresses laid on a wooden plank raised by concrete blocks. The sides and head of the spartan provisional bed touched three walls in the room. There was just enough space between the foot of the bed and the fourth wall to allow for a small wicker dresser with a twenty-four-inch flatscreen TV on top. Joy faced the TV. It was blaring. Some action movie. She didn't remember it being on when she went to bed. But she didn't remember much at that moment, and she was still unclear as to where she was. She did remember Jake. She felt queasy again as she thought of him, and she forced herself to breathe. There was an explosion. (On the TV.) A steroided cartoon of a "man" opened fire with a shotgun he held with one hand. Funny how ballistic recoil never seemed to exist in these cartoon men's worlds. Joy cocked her head and wondered why she found herself thinking of ballistic recoil. She'd never held a gun in her life.

She turned the TV off. On her left was a small window close to the ceiling, and Joy could see grass and weeds and concrete pavement at the window's level outside. Was she in a basement? Her heart sped up in panic. Why was she in a basement? To her right was a small doorway with no door. She passed through, and into what appeared to be a miniature living room replete with a studio sofa and a small, rectangular, industrial-style coffee table. Her heart slowed. Jake was on the sofa, his legs uncomfortably dangling over the sofa's arm, his own arm uncomfortably spilling onto the nearby coffee table.

Joy sat on the edge of the table. She remembered now. They had promised to stick together. No matter what. He had asked if they should go to her place or his. She said his. She did not say there was no longer a hers. They came here, to his basement apartment. She flopped on the bed immediately. He said he'd take the couch. She told him it was okay, he should sleep in his bed. He ignored her and shut the lights off. She wished he would lay beside her, but she was too tired to voice this desire. She fell asleep.

Wide awake now, Joy stared at the sleeping face, framed by the chicken suit, of the soft-breathing, traditionally handsome male before her. He had full Cupid's bow lips and dark curls that poked out from beneath the suit's red comb. He had a bit of a belly, but that was okay.

"He's younger than I am," Joy muttered. "He shouldn't have a belly."

He had a bit of a belly, but that was okay. A healthy diet and some regular jogging could slim that right down.

Jake's hand smashed against the coffee table, startling Joy. His eyelids sprung open, the sphincter muscles of his irises contracting as he scanned the room and let his pupils rest on Joy, whose face now hovered above his.

"Hypnagogic jerk," she said with her hand over her mouth to shield him from the exudation of her morning breath.

"I'm not a—" Jake said, his hand over his mouth as well.

"No, you had a—"

"Please stop calling me a jerk."

"I didn't mean…"

"What happened to meaning without being mean?"

Joy perked her head toward the sound of the cartoon man on the television killing something, then saying a funny one-liner. Hadn't she turned the TV off? She changed the subject. "What were you dreaming about?" she asked. "Were you falling?"

"No," Jake said with a faraway stare. "Everything was falling around me."

Joy squinted as she gazed into the infinite expanse behind his eyes. "Yeah," she said simply. "Yeah," he said back. Joy stood and returned to the bedroom. There was another explosion. She turned the TV off. Jake took the opportunity to run into the bathroom and shut the door. "What's the plan today?" he heard her say. He stood before his bathroom mirror and stared into his own eyes with dread.

Now, the dread itself wasn't the problem. It was the *source* of the dread that particularly irked him this morning. See, he normally felt dread every morning in his bathroom, as this was the time he reserved to pull the trigger of his empty pistol while holding it to his temple. Each morning, he dreaded it would be the morning he finally put a round in the chamber. He also dreaded it would be yet another morning he did not put a round in the chamber. Sometimes, he dreaded he didn't conduct a proper safety check and there was already a round in the chamber. And other times, he dreaded the click of the firing pin once again stabbing the thin air of a disappointingly empty chamber. This morning was different. This morning, the source of Jake's dread was neither of those things. This morning, the source of said dread was the expansion of his colon past its limit to accommodate the byproducts of food digested at least three days ago, resulting in the involuntary relaxation of both his internal and external anal sphincters—leading to the process commonly referred to as "turtle-heading"—which would in and of itself not be a problem; the problem, and the main component of Jake's overwhelming dread, was he still hadn't figured out how to remove his chicken suit.

"What are we going to do today, Jake?" Joy asked again.

"Same thing we do every day, Joy," he answered through the door while frantically searching for a button or a zipper in vain. "Try to figure out the world."

"Good plan," Joy said. "I think we should start with the Ice Cream Man."

Jake raised his arms and tugged at the suit from his shoulders. This too was done in vain. What was also in vain was his attempt to cease the colonic peristalsis his nervous system had initiated. "Ponth J. Sahib?" he answered as he broke into a sweat and gave up and sat on the toilet with his suit still on.

"Yeah, him," said Joy. "Let's go find him."

Jake's face contorted in agonized pleasure, or pleasured agony, as his vagus nerve, pudendal nerve, and prostatic plexus fired signals in waves. He decided in that moment of blissful connection with all that is good and true and right in the world to simply ask Joy to pass a knife through the door so he could cut the suit off.

But then, with simultaneous confusion and relief, he heard a plop resound in the toilet, followed by the peaceful cadence of a burbling creek as his bladder joined his bowels in the expunging of its contents.

"What if he wasn't real?" Jake called out and snatched a wad of toilet paper and discovered, to great satisfaction, that he could not only relieve, but clean himself as well.

"He's real," said Joy.

Jake flushed the toilet, stood, stretched his arms, went to the sink and washed his feathered hands. "Dude shows up out of nowhere singing his ice cream truck song, helps us fight a bunch of guys with no faces, then jumps out a window and disappears." He toweled his hands, opened the door, and stepped out. "What if he was just a figment of our imagination?"

"Was it our imagination?" Joy said, standing in the kitchenette and leaning against the refrigerator.

"I think it might have—"

"But was it *our* imagination. Not your imagination. Not mine. Ours."

"That's what I'm thinking."

Joy smiled. "Then he was real."

Jake shook his head. "I don't know. Maybe, someway..."

The sound of a knock interrupted him. Joy looked around. "Where's that coming from?"

"Upstairs," Jake said. "Probably my landlord."

Joy followed Jake as he walked from the kitchenette to a door in the living room. When he opened this door, there was a flight of stairs to the left that only led up. They ascended those stairs to another door, which was knocked upon once more by whoever was on the other side.

Jake opened the door to a flood of light and the familiar Botox smile of his landlord. "Hi," the Landlord said. "Didn't mean to bother." He smiled at Joy, who smiled back. "Your friends were looking for you."

Jake and Joy's eyes adjusted and the two individuals standing beside the Landlord came into view. The first was a tall woman with dusky features not quite aquiline, but certainly not bovine, ovine, ursine, or porcine. Definitely not elaphine. Maybe a bit anserine or corvine. The second individual was...

"Ponth!" Joy said, and rushed to hug him.

"Hey, little chicken." Ponth hugged her back, then nodded at the statuesque woman beside him. "I brought reinforcements. This is Sarah." He peered at Jake. "You gonna invite us in?"

***

Let's rewind a bit.

Ponth and Sarah showed up at Jake's door after Jake resolved his bowel issues after Joy woke up in a fog after Jake and Joy spoke to Y—who rambled about eggs, lamb shifts, and Eeyore—after Jake and Joy noticed everyone on their train was hypnotized after they launched a simultaneous worldview attack after Ponth jumped out of the hospital room window and... (PLAY!)

After Ponth jumped out of the hospital room window, he sprinted through downtown avenues crowded with retail clerks and bank tellers and real estate attorneys, crowded with municipal gas line repair workers and restaurant staff on cigarette breaks smoking beside pitched tents arranged on the sidewalks by the houseless like eyots in a human gyre. An itinerant squatted outside a vestibule in the middle of the crowd, pushed a considerable length of feces from their anus and screamed, *"Follow Meeee! I am your God!"*

A car honked, and Ponth's ears would not have distinguished it from the cacophony of vehicular horns had it not been followed by the sharp report of a woman shouting his name. *"Ponth!"* Sarah screamed from her rolled-down window as she pulled her car over (a beige early-2000s Buick Century—did that detail matter? We can do whatever we want!) on the opposite side of the street. Ponth locked eyes on her, then plunged into traffic. A high-end Mercedes screeched to a halt. "The fuck is wrong with you!" the driver screamed. "Fuck you, one-percenter!" Ponth screamed back, dodging a motorcycle. "I'm not a..." the Mercedes driver stammered, then shouted, "This is a certified pre-owned lease with a prepaid maintenance option that I work very hard for, asshole!"

"Hey, you're right," Ponth called back as he jumped into Sarah's Buick. "I'm sorry. You're clearly in a lot of pain and I just made your day worse."

"My heart hurts!" the Mercedes driver exploded. "Every day it hurts *so* much and the keyless ignition, leather steering wheel, and dual climate control makes me feel *just a little bit better!"*

"Go, go, go," Ponth said to Sarah. "Can't deal with this poor soul right now."

Sarah hit the gas and merged back into traffic. "You need to stop doing that."

"I'm not doing it," Ponth said. From behind, they heard the Mercedes driver still shouting, *"And no one understands me better than the remote access services app it comes with!"*

Sarah turned left to get away from the Mercedes. "That is the third time this week I've seen you indiscriminately induce an existential crisis."

"It's not me!"

"Hey," she said. "Check your ego at the door. We don't want Hip Gnosis getting eyes on us."

"Hip Gnosis already has eyes on us. Assume we're being surveilled right now."

Sarah turned another corner. "Then let's lead them on a nothing chase. Tank is full, let's head for the border."

"No. Head back to the hospital. We're keeping an eye on the Chickens."

"If they escaped, we'll lead Hip Gnosis directly to them."

"If they escaped, then the launching end of the offensive is where we stay."

Sarah stopped at a red light. "And you're the one always warning me about being overaggressive."

"The Twin Chickens are here."

"You're certain of that?"

"I saw them. They are real. I confirmed it with my own soul windows."

"Your soul… ?"

"My eyes, Sarah. Stay with me. I was referring to my—"

"Maybe stick to the tactical stuff, Shakespeare."

"Tactically, the Twin Chickens change everything."

"If they're the real deal."

"They're the real deal on wheels of steel. Why do you think we keep seeing these spontaneous existential crises?"

The light turned green, but Sarah didn't take her foot off the brake. Instead, she glared at Ponth, who looked away. He couldn't maintain eye contact when she looked at him like that. It made him feel like he was falling into an abyss.

The car behind them honked. Sarah ignored it. "How old are you now, Ponth?"

"Oh, jeez… I've lost…"

"You are a very wise, very experienced man."

"Thank you?"

"You are rightfully head of tactical operations, and I have always respected the chain of command."

Drivers from behind sped angrily around their stalled Buick. Ponth pointed at the green light. "We should maybe…"

"But I am telling you this as… I love you as a friend and I love you like a son. Or a grandson. Or a great-grandson. Or a great-great—"

"I get it."

"I am only saying, I've seen, with *my* own eyes, a lot of wise and experienced men lose themselves in their wisdom and their experience."

"Then doubt me," said Ponth. "Doubt my word. Come meet the Chickens yourself."

The light turned red. Sarah touched her foot to the gas and ran through it. Ponth groaned.

Then, a static-filled female voice came in over the car's two-way radio. "Sarah. Hailee. A male and female just ran out the front entrance of Saint Veronica's. Looks like they're heading for the waterfront."

Sarah grabbed the handset of her radio. "Description?"

"The cherry blossoms have bloomed throughout the waterfront park, along the river that runs north between two mountain ranges that—"

"Of the male and female," Sarah snapped. Ponth chuckled.

"Male's just intensely moving forward. Female keeps flapping her arms and screaming she wants to fly."

"That's them," Ponth said. Sarah peered at him. Ponth shrugged. "We'll do what you want to do."

"Stay on them, Hailee," Sarah said into her radio.

"You got it, Boss. They're almost at the waterfront."

"We'll catch up." Sarah made another left, then sped east, toward the murky river that cut through the city, now visible a few blocks ahead. When they reached the parkway that ran parallel to the river, they hit a red light, and Sarah grabbed her handset again. "We're on the waterfront."

Ponth mumbled. "I coulda been a contend—"

"Stop it," said Sarah.

"Looks like they're headed for the bridge," said Hailee on the radio.

"Which one?" asked Sarah.

"The pretty reddish-orange one. I'd bet anything that's a truss design, with a double-leaf, Rall-type bascule lift—"

"Stay on them," Sarah said. The light turned green. She turned left and raced north up the parkway. Ponth smiled.

"Yes, ma'am," Hailee said back.

***

Madelyne placed a heavy gray box studded with buttons, dials, and light-emitting diodes on Hip Gnosis's desk. Gnosis, still facing his window, watched the nothingness of night blanket the corporate campus. "Whaaaaat," he said without turning, "is that beastly, anachronistic contraption?"

Madelyne crouched under his desk, running a wired plug into a floor outlet. "A radio dispatch console. You need to receive updates in real-time."

"Don't they have software for that?"

Madelyne stood and slammed her palm on the desk. Hip Gnosis froze. "I've upset you," he said.

Madelyne turned the console on. The diodes lit up. "Babies with bad tummies get upset," she said quietly, then turned a dial. "Software can freeze. These anachronistic contraptions are far more reliable."

"How we doing?" Hip Gnosis asked.

Madelyne pushed a button. "Ask them yourself."

"Alrighty then," Hip Gnosis said, then called out in a playful falsetto, "What's up, my ninjaaaaas! This is the Boss with the Sauce, the Chief of Belief, the Narrative Executive of the Effective Collectiiiiiiive."

"Sir," a voice said from the console. "We're maintaining visual on WVFF personnel."

"How many do you see?"

"Two vehicles. They've been following the Chickens all night."

"Aaaand who's in the vehicles?"

"We've only been able to positively ID one subject. Sahib. Ponth J.—"

"Ugh," Hip Gnosis said. "Any chance Ponth and his crew

swung by anything resembling a C3?"

"Negative. They followed the Chickens to a residence on the east side a few hours ago. They're still there."

"Still where?"

"At the residence. WVFF has been sitting outside in their vehicles."

"So that's where the Chickens live."

"Likely. We passed the address to Madelyne."

"Well… that's a promising consolation prize. Tell me about the residence. Building? Complex?"

"Standalone, single-family home. Victorian. Tree-lined street."

"Suhhhweeeet! Find the utility poles near the house and forward their locations to Madelyne. PUH-EAACE!"

"Copy. Over and out."

"Madelyne, switch to alpha-four please."

Madelyne turned a knob, then pressed a button. "Go ahead."

"Yo yo YO!" Gnosis shouted.

"Miscommunication Unit. Standing by," a new voice from the console replied.

"Soooooo," said Hip Gnosis. "Remember that thing that time that I didn't not talk to you about somewhere after oh, I don't know… ?"

"Okay, sure," the console said. "We can say we mostly, somewhat, recall that, I think. Yeah."

***

A thin line of drool traveled from Ponth's lower lip to his collarbone as he dreamed of a little girl standing on the side of a highway, screaming at a plume of smoke in the distance crawling like a serpent toward the heavens. "*No fueron ellos!*" the girl screamed. "Por favor escucha! Fui yo!" Ponth reached for her, thinking to hold her and calm her down, but the world trembled and his knee smashed into the glove compartment in Sarah's Buick and he snapped awake.

"Wipe your face," Sarah said, still sitting in the driver's seat and reading a newspaper.

"I miss anything?" Ponth mumbled, wiping his mouth with his sleeve.

"You snore."

"Little chilly in here," he said. The windows were cracked open, and the air conditioning roared at full blast.

"You fart too."

Ponth squinted at the morning sun. His eyes meandered to Sarah's reading material: a thin local weekly she had opened to a full-page color ad for a Spiritually Uplifting Communal and Destiny Intensifying Conference to be held at the downtown waterfront park in two days. He tapped his finger on the page, hitting the face of a smiling bald monk in red-and-yellow robes, and said, "This guy."

Sarah moved the paper out of his reach. "One thing at a time."

"Now who is that?" Ponth said, and pointed toward the Victorian house they were surveilling down the block.

"Who?"

"That. There. On the pole."

Sarah followed the imaginary line from Ponth's finger to the utility pole a few houses down from the Victorian. Someone in a white hard hat and neon-orange mesh vest climbed the pole. "I don't know," Sarah said. "Cable guy?"

"Anyone else notice that?"

"Doesn't look too—"

"Jesus..."

Sarah calmly rolled up the windows, then suddenly boomed, "DON'T YOU DARE INVOKE THAT NAME AGAINST ME!" Her thundering voice shook the whole car.

Ponth covered his ears. "Take it easy. It's just an expression in this era."

"You know how many fucked-up expressions I've heard over how many fucked-up eras?"

"I know, Sarah, I'm—"

"Here's my favorite: Os certifico que con la ayuda de Dios entraré poderosamente contra vosotros y os haré guerra por todos las partes y maneras que tuviere..." She gripped the steering wheel and gritted her teeth. "These. Fucking. People."

Ponth let out a long breath. "These people are doing the best they can."

"They need to do better."

"I've a feeling they're about to start." Ponth grabbed the handset of the Buick's two-way radio. "Teaching moment here, team. See that pole? That's not a cable guy. That's the enemy."

The radio crackled. "Darn it. Sorry, Boss."

"It's okay, Hailee. Learn the lesson and move on. But the Chickens aren't safe. The enemy's made their move. Now we make ours."

He handed the radio back to Sarah and unlocked his door.

"You want to fill us in on said move, Mr. Mystery?" Sarah said.

"Yeah, yeah, sorry." He took the radio back.

"Were you having a senior moment there? Or you just get caught up in the moment?"

"Little bit of both," he said, then spoke into the radio, "Peel off. Meet us back at HQ."

"You sure, Boss?" a male voice came in on the radio this time. "They'll be following us."

"Call Azrael," Ponth said. "They'll help you take a secure countersurveillance route."

"Will do."

Ponth opened the passenger-side door. Sarah scoffed. "You still haven't told us—"

"Ready to meet the Chickens?" he said.

Sarah shook her head. "Sure."

They got out of the Buick and shut its doors. "Don't sound so excited," Ponth said as they headed for the Victorian.

"Ask me again," said Sarah.

"Ready to meet the—"

"Damn skippy!"

Ponth chuckled as they reached the Victorian and walked up its steps to the porch.

"That's an expression from this era I do like," said Sarah.

"It's a good one. Little outdated."

"It's not that old."

"It's kind of old."

"Things keep changing faster and faster." Sarah sighed. Ponth pushed the doorbell on the porch and watched the climber on the utility pole from the corner of his eye. Hip Gnosis's agents wouldn't take aggressive action out in the open. Still, they needed to be ready for anything.

A man in jeans and flip-flops opened the door. He looked as if he hadn't slept in weeks. He tensed as if he was about to shut the door and rush back inside. Ponth and Sarah blinked. He relaxed a little. "Hi," he said with caution.

Sarah cocked an eyebrow at Ponth.

Ponth stammered. "Maybe, sorry, I think we got the wrong…"

"Were you looking for Jake?" the man said.

"Yep." Ponth brightened.

"I'm his landlord. He has his own entrance. Come on, I'll show you."

The Landlord led them around the side of the house. Ponth glanced toward the utility pole. The climber was gone. "Sorry to bother you," Sarah said.

"No worries," said the Landlord. They reached a door on the side of the house. The Landlord knocked.

The screech of car tires pierced the peaceful morning air. Ponth and Sarah stiffened and looked toward the street as two vehicles accelerated by. The Landlord shook his head. "Stupid," he said. "Kids play on this street. I'd bring it up to the neighborhood association but what does it matter if the city council erases the association from the Civics Code like it's planning? And now they want to turn the derelict house around the corner… you know where all the squatters go to camp out and shoot up? Been complaining about that for years. City does nothing. Police do nothing. Now the city wants to use my taxes to turn it into a shelter so the same people can continue to camp out and shoot up and the cops can continue to do nothing. Same difference. Now you've just got hard-working people paying for the renovation. But you know what the kicker of it all is? That isn't why I'm grumbling so much. I'm grumbling because I'm lonely and heartbroken and it's just easier to talk about all the problems of local governance or lack thereof instead of what's really going on inside." The Landlord knocked on the door again, and Sarah looked sternly at Ponth, who muttered, "Telling you, it's not me."

Jake and Joy answered the door.

"Ponth!" Joy said, and rushed to hug him.

"Hey, little chicken." Ponth hugged her back. "I brought reinforcements. This is Sarah," he said. Then he peered at Jake. "You gonna invite us in?"

CHAPTER 5

Jake and Joy winced. Not from Ponth's request to invite him in, but from the vituperative soliloquy sullenly vomited by the Landlord.

Now hold on just one cotton-picking… hey, whoa, let's not say cotton-picking… hold on just one darn minute, the voice of narrative continuity declares. Said soliloquy was vomited *before* Jake and Joy answered the door. How did they hear it?

Well, they didn't need to hear it. They *saw* it. See, when Jake and Joy opened the door, what they saw was:

1.) a short, swarthy, highly energetic man who previously identified himself as a Sahib-motherfucker-Ponth-J-Sahib;

2.) a tall, quietly intense woman subsequently identified by the Sahib-motherfucker-Ponth-J-Sahib as a reinforcements-this-is-Sarah;

and

3.) Jake's landlord, whose clothes were covered with greenish vomit that dripped to the ground.

A light breeze blew the smell of bile toward Jake and Joy. They winced again. Joy tugged at the feathers of Jake's elbow and said, "Can you read it?"

Jake nodded, scanning the strings of letters he saw in the Landlord's trickling vomit. "Yeah. I'm up to '… the city wants to use my taxes to turn it into a shelter…'"

"I finished reading it already," Joy said with pride.

"Well good for you, Will Hunting. Sorry I'm not used to speed-reading vomit."

"Jerk."

"I'm not a…" he said, then ignored her and continued to read.

Sarah laughed with tears in her eyes. She covered her mouth with her hands and tried to regain self-control. "They *are* the real deal on wheels of steel."

"Told you." Ponth smiled. Joy began to cry.

"Why are you crying, sweety?" Sarah asked.

"I don't know," Joy blubbered. "Because you are?"

Sarah grabbed the far smaller Joy into a hug and stroked the back of her neck. "It's okay. I know you're really confused right now."

"... lack thereof instead of what's really going on inside!" Jake said proudly as he finally finished reading the Landlord's vomit. But then his face became sad and pained. "Not all the people in and out that house are bad all the time, you know. Some are families. With kids sometimes. Or they lost their families or they lost their, they maybe lost their kids, right? They're trying to survive. Or maybe they're just, I don't know... just *trying*."

The Landlord's expression mirrored the pain in Jake's, and he clutched his abdomen and retched.

Joy, still in Sarah's arms, mumbled into the taller woman's bosom, "We should move over a bit."

Jake and Ponth stepped back with the two women. The Landlord vomited again.

Jake struggled to read the sentences swimming in the streaming spew. "I'm... sorry... I'm still... not..."

"I think he needs your help," Sarah whispered in Joy's ear.

"You remind me of my mom," Joy mumbled. "She was tall like you."

"Well, I'm kind of like, *the* mother figure, so..."

"... over... it..." Jake said.

"He needs you," Sarah said again.

Joy stomped her foot and detached from a warmth she hadn't experienced since she was five years old. She stepped over to Jake and the sorrowful Landlord and read the bile pooled on the pavement:

"I'm sorry, I'm still not over it. It's been eight years since I lost my Anna and I still cry every morning of every day when I wake up and that fog of dreams lifts and I remember she's gone. People say it gets better and I guess it has. I don't think as much about sitting in my car in the garage and leaving it on. That's a lie, I still think about it. I know she's out there somewhere, in a different form or energy or what have you. I *know* this. But she's still gone. And the pain of that sears away any knowing or any comforting thoughts. It sears away any faith. Anna, she used to tell me, she used to say 'You have to collect smiles.' And she'd hold my hand when we took our walks through the city. She loved to walk. Especially now, in the spring, with all the cherry blossoms about to bloom. She'd count, one, two, three, four – she'd count every time we passed someone who smiled at us. I'd tell her 'Honey, human beings are a crazy species, stop being so nice to everyone, you've got to stop.' And she'd ignore me, and she'd keep smiling. She'd smile at the squatters over there too. She'd give them money. I'd be so worried and so angry. I'd tell her 'One of those guys is gonna follow you home one day when I'm not around and murder you.' She'd ignore me. That's not what killed her anyway. Liver cancer did it. Liver cancer."

Joy looked up briefly at everyone. "New paragraph," she whispered sadly, then continued.

"Do you have any idea how healthy that woman ate? And she walked everywhere, every day. She was fifty-two and before the cancer hit, she looked ten years younger. Yesterday, she would have turned sixty. We had plans. We were going to walk all over the world. We were going to grow old together, traveling. We ate healthy, she made me. We saved money, I made her. We were nice to everyone, she made me do that too. We did everything right. We did everything right and we still got shafted. She's dead. And I'm here, alone. So I see those people shooting up with their needles, and I wonder how it is they get to be here and she doesn't? How is it their livers still function and hers wouldn't? I'm not mad at them. I don't hate them. I'm just, very confused."

Joy finished reading and the Landlord muttered, "I'm sorry. I shouldn't vomit all over you like this. You've got your friends here."

"No, I'm..." Jake started. "I didn't know... all that."

"I never told you," the Landlord said, reverting to his beaming Botox smile.

Joy stared at the vomit in silence. Sarah and Ponth stood awkwardly. And Jake, well... he felt as if his eyeballs had retreated into his head and were now ricocheting about the cavern of his empty skull in a desperate search for a string of words that could prove soothing or profound or, at the very least, appropriate. He glanced at Joy in the hope of receiving some measure of assistance, but Joy, her red comb flaccid, was clearly experiencing the same difficulty.

Jake's eyes, still bouncing around his head, found words only to reject them. There was *sorry*, but this word was unnecessary, for Jake possessed no blame or unmet responsibility. There was *condolences*, but this word, coming to him from the Latin *dolere* and *con*, felt disingenuous—for Jake was not *suffering with* the Landlord, he barely knew him.

These words were useless.

As such, Jake's eyes shifted to the scanning of recalled, pertinent statistics. There were close to eight billion people in the world. Approximately one hundred and fifty thousand of these people died every day. Contrary to what he believed when he was a younger man, terrorism and war were not the leading causes of these deaths; said causes only accounted for less than 1 percent of said deaths. The leading causes, in order from least to most responsible, were tuberculosis, diarrhea, road injuries, diabetes, lung cancer, dementia, lower respiratory disease, pulmonary disease, stroke, and finally—heading the pack with a distant lead—ischemic disease of the heart.

But these numbers, too, were useless.

Jake looked once more to Joy for help. But Joy, having sensed Jake was considering fatalities from war and terrorism, added natural disasters to this tragic list and became lost in a triggered memory of cinderblock dust and her mother's fading warmth. This, in turn, triggered Jake's memory of that massive, rolling cloud of gypsum particles chasing him and a crowd into St. Peter's Roman Catholic Church.

"All we can do," said Joy, breaking their engendered remembrance and looking to the Landlord, not with suffering, but with passion, "is pray."

But at this, Jake clenched his feathered fists and spat on the ground. "Fuck prayer."

The Landlord looked from Joy to Jake and back again, his artificial smile frozen in place. Then, as crisply as one participating in a military changing of the guard, he turned a hundred and eighty degrees and walked back to the front porch of the Victorian home.

"Wait..." Joy called out weakly. But the Landlord had already disappeared around the corner. She then looked at Jake with a mixture of concern and disappointment in her eyes.

Jake avoided her gaze and leaned against the side trim of his door. "I let you guys in," he said to Ponth and Sarah, "it's under the condition you explain what the hell is going on."

"Young man," Sarah said, "I don't care who or what you are, you don't dictate—"

"Done, Jake," Ponth broke in, touching Sarah's arm. "Come on. Let's go inside and talk."

***

In his subterranean domicile, Jake pointed at his studio sofa and said to his guests, "Please." Ponth nodded and sat. Sarah pushed her hands into her jean jacket pockets and said, "I'll stand." Joy looked up at Sarah and fought the overwhelming urge to hug her again. Jake looked up at her and fought the overwhelming urge to salute.

"Before I forget," Sarah said, pulling her smartphone from her pants pocket. She tapped and swiped at the screen, then held the phone out at arm's length, meandering through the apartment. She eventually found her way to the bedroom.

"What's she... ?" Jake looked at Ponth.

"Scanning for ELSUR," Ponth said.

Joy pointed toward the kitchenette and giggled. "El sur es por ahí. ¿A dónde vamos?"

"Not el sur, pollita." Ponth laughed in kind. "ELSUR..."

"Electronic surveillance," Jake grumbled. "Enough with the word games."

"Seems clear," Sarah said as she rejoined them in the living room.

"Let's get to the point," Jake said.

"*This is the poynt,*" Joy bellowed. "*To speken short and pleyn!*"

"Chicken suits," said Jake, ignoring Joy's outburst. "That

we can't take off."

"If you say so, tough guy," said Sarah.

"Never-ending stairs," Jake continued. "Faceless men…"

"Might meet some faceless women too," said Ponth.

"Don't forget the swirly, hypnotized eyes," Joy said.

"That *was* creepy," Jake agreed, then pointed to Joy. "And she always knows what's going on in my head."

"Not always," Joy protested. "Only when you think out loud."

"I never think out loud."

"You do too! I hear your thinking, but like, someone else is thinking also? You, but not you, and that's when you're thinking out loud, but…" Joy flapped her feathered arms in frustration.

Jake gestured toward her as if to say "see what I'm dealing with?"

"I have to deal with you too!" Joy responded to his unspoken thought. He gestured toward her again.

"Wow," Sarah said. Ponth chuckled. Then Jake said, "She also did a weird, real-life, split-screen thing."

Ponth and Sarah perked up. "Real-life, split-screen… ?" Sarah asked.

"We both did that!" Joy shouted. "It took both of us. You just followed my lead."

"Weird, split-screen… ?" Ponth asked as well.

"After you jumped out the window," Jake told Ponth. "That's how we escaped the hospital. She—"

"We!" said Joy.

"She and me made, I don't know…"

"I was able to see both," Joy tried to explain. "I saw we could do both."

"Did you guys do two different things at the same time that felt like you were only doing one thing?" Ponth asked. Jake and Joy nodded vigorously. Ponth and Sarah traded a look.

"Unbelievable," Sarah said.

"Told you," Ponth responded. "Look how quick they figured out how to do that."

"Do what?" asked Jake.

"How long have you two been awake?" Sarah ignored his question.

"Awake?" said Jake.

"A day," Ponth answered, jumping to his feet from the sofa. "They've been awake a day and they've already figured out how to use their worldview to manipulate quantum stochastic processes."

Sarah shook her head. "And here I was impressed with how they merged time-space compression with the manifestation of a metaphor."

"Time-space... ?" said Jake.

"That's what you did when you were reading the vomit," answered Ponth.

"Joy did most of that," grumbled Jake.

"I did." Joy beamed.

"You did," said Ponth.

Joy stretched her arms and did a pirouette. "I. Am. Awesome."

"What happened to 'we'?" Jake muttered.

"Oh, stop," said Joy.

Ponth chuckled. Sarah folded her arms. "Come on," Ponth said, gazing up at her stern expression. "You believe me now, right?"

"I do," Sarah responded. "We should take them to Levi."

"Agreed," said Ponth. He turned to Jake and Joy. "Ready for a field trip?"

Joy nodded.

"No," said Jake.

"I thought you wanted answers," said Ponth.

"Who the hell is Levi?"

"Hey, you will dig Levi. Trust me."

"I *don't* trust you, Ice Cream Man. You said you would come in and give us answers. Thus far, none have been forthcoming."

"All this stuff is complicated, big guy," Ponth replied. "And Levi is the WVFF personnel—"

"*W*, *V*, who?"

"Sorry, acronyms… Look, Levi's the one especially trained for explaining things to the newbies."

"Why don't you explain things, Sahib-motherfucker-Ponth-J-Sahib?" said Jake.

"Because," Ponth said patiently, "they need to be explained a certain way to you. You two are… different."

Jake sat on his sofa. Joy sat beside him. "It can't hurt," she said.

"How do you know?" he replied.

"Come on." She grabbed his feathered arm and tugged. "This is supposed to be an adventure."

Jake considered her words as she annoyingly pulled at his arm again and again. "Fine," he relented. "Just stop. Where's this Levi?"

Ponth clapped his palms together. "HQ. Let's go."

"We can't go out there," said Sarah. "Hip Gnosis's surveillance will be all over us."

"Of course," Ponth said with a grin. He walked over to the bathroom door, pulled out a smartphone, and tapped its screen.

"No," Sarah said. "No. You are not opening a wormhole here."

"You got a better option?"

"Every time you use one of those, it depletes our operating budget by at least five percent and finance has a fit."

Ponth placed his smartphone on the floor by the closed bathroom door. "Finance can lick my—"

"The Stakeholders won't be happy."

"The Stakeholders are trapped in Eternity."

Jake and Joy shared a perplexed glance. A robotic voice emitted from Ponth's phone. "Please state your full name for authorization."

"Ponth J. Sahib."

"Transaction authorized. Confirmation code: P… Q… 3…"

Ponth fumbled with his jacket pockets. "Anybody got a pen? Paper?"

"7… J… R… 2…"

"It's good to write these down," said Ponth while everyone

looked around in a disingenuous attempt to find pen and paper they knew they didn't have.

"S... 4... 3..."

"Did they say *S* 4 or *F* 4?"

"5... 8. To initiate Einstein-Rosen Bridge, press or say one. To cancel this transaction, press or say two. To use a different account, press or say..."

"Listen." Ponth faced Jake and Joy. "We're taking you into the heart of our command and control center. So I need you guys to check your egos at the door."

Jake folded his arms with a skeptical squint. "Okay."

Joy shrugged. "I have no ego."

"... To repeat these options, press or say five."

"Five," Ponth said, then turned his attention to Joy. "I need you to understand this. If your egos rear their ugly little heads while we're at HQ, Hip Gnosis can potentially track their signals to our C3. All egos transmit directly to and from him."

"Hypnosis?" Jake asked.

"He'd have billions of signals to weed through," Sarah chimed in. "Unlikely he'd isolate yours. Still... not a chance we can take."

"Hypnosis is a... person?" asked Joy.

"Not exactly," Ponth replied. "Either way, he's incredibly dangerous. So we, literally, need you to check your egos at the door. You got anything on your mind threatening those monstrous little things, come out with it now."

"Seriously?" said Jake.

"As cancer," Ponth answered.

"... To repeat these options," said the phone by the bathroom door, "press or say—"

"Five!" said Ponth. "Out with it, Jake. Please."

"Alright, well..." Jake shook his head. "I'm pissed Joy seems able to figure all this stuff out so quickly. I don't know what's going on, and I'm confused, and everything is just coming to her naturally. I feel, you know... useless."

At this, a winged bat-monkey-cherub creature silently appeared at his feet. "Ah!" Joy exclaimed in horror, then stomped on it. It disappeared with a *poof*.

"Did she just stomp out his ego?" Sarah muttered to Ponth.

"I think so," Ponth muttered back.

Jake smiled. "Huh. That does feel better."

Joy lost her breath again. "That is the first time I've seen you smile."

They locked eyes. Jake looked away. "You've seen me smile before."

"I have not."

"Didn't we share a laugh on the bridge?"

"A very sardonic laugh."

"Your turn, Joy," Ponth broke in.

"I don't have..." Joy protested.

"... To repeat these options—"

"Five. Joy, I can't keep cycling through the options."

"There's nothing..."

"Please, Joy," said Sarah. "This is real."

"But..."

"Come on," said Ponth.

"Fine!" Joy stamped her foot, and her rear toe clicked against the gray ceramic tile of the basement living room. "I don't think Jake is attracted to me!"

Jake looked at the floor and blushed. Sarah and Ponth shifted nervously. A bat-monkey-cherub appeared on Joy's left shoulder, giggled, and did a pirouette.

"Get it off! Get it off!" Joy shrieked.

Jake rushed to grab a throw pillow off his sofa. "Hold still!"

Sarah shook her head. "Their metaphor manifestations are insanely strong."

Jake swung the pillow with full force and hit the little ego monster. It too vanished with a *poof*. Unfortunately, he hit Joy in the face as well.

"Oy!" Jake exclaimed as Joy slumped to the floor. He knelt beside her. "I am so, so sorry."

"... To repeat these options—"

"One!" said Ponth.

"Are you okay?" Jake asked Joy.

"That wasn't on purpose, right?" she responded.

"Course not."

"Einstein-Rosen Bridge initiated in three, two..." said Ponth's smartphone.

"Let's go, Chickens," Ponth said.

Jake took Joy's hand and helped her to her feet. They locked eyes again. Jake held her gaze this time and stammered, "And you are, really pretty. I just..." He waved his hand around his comb and feather-framed face. "There's a lot going on in there."

Joy nodded and gripped his hand tighter. He squeezed her grip back.

"We gotta do this now," said Ponth.

"Where's this bridge?" said Jake.

"Here." Ponth opened the bathroom door and entered. Sarah followed.

Joy scrunched her face. "When's the last time you cleaned in there?"

***

From his office, Hip Gnosis stood facing his floor-to-ceiling window, watching the morning sun hover over his corporate campus. Madelyne stood at his desk.

"What's happening, my peopleeeees!" Gnosis shouted. Madelyne cringed. The radio dispatch console on his desk squawked. "Still no movement."

Hip Gnosis put his hands on his hips and took a deep breath. "Whaaaaaaaaaaaaaaaaaaaaaaaaaaaaaaaaaaaaaa
aaaaaaaaaaaaaaaaaaaaaaaaaaaaaaaaaaaaaaaaaaaaaaa
aaaaaaaaaaaaaaaaaaaaaaaaaaaaaaaaaaaaaaaaaaaaaaa
aaaaaaaaaaaaaaaaaaaaaaaaaaaaaaaaaaaaaaaaaaaaaaa
aaaaaaaaaaaaaaaaaaaaaaaaaaaaaaaaaaaaaaaaaaaaaaa
aaaaaaaaaaaaaaaaaaaaaaaat? How long's it been now?"

"About five hours, sir," the voice from the console answered. "No one's come back out since Ponth and the woman with him went in."

"That's crazy town, y'all. Madelyne, switch to alpha-four."

Madelyne reached for the console.

"Wait, sir. Wait," the console said.

"Yes?" said Hip Gnosis.

"That woman, the one with Ponth. Not a hundred percent sure, but… we think it's Sarah."

Hip Gnosis's head burst into flames again.

"Goddamn it," Madelyne said, and stepped back from the heat.

"*THE* SARAH?" Hip Gnosis asked in booming surround sound.

"We think so," said the console.

"NOT SARAH JESSICA PARKER OR SARAH MICHELLE GELLAR OR SARAH THE DUCHESS OF FUCKING YORK. *THE* SARAH?"

"We think so," the console repeated.

"EXIT THE AREA. WE'RE WASTING TIME AND RESOURCES. PONTH'S JUDGMENT? ALWAYS BEEN SUSPECT. BUT SARAH, SHE WON'T BE STUPID ENOUGH TO LET YOU SEE HER AGAIN ON THEIR WAY OUT."

"Copy. Over."

"AM I GOING TO HAVE ANY ISSUES WITH WHAT I JUST SAID?" Gnosis asked Madelyne.

"No. You're right. Sarah would never be so careless as to—"

"NO, I MEAN THE—"

"Could you just… turn down the flames? And the voice?"

"Sorry," he said at a normal volume. The flames withered away. "You know I get a little impassioned sometimes."

"You can get impassioned without spontaneously combusting."

"You're right."

"It's okay."

"I meant my Sarah comments. Any issues there?"

"What, because you… ? No, you just mentioned them in passing. You didn't say anything slanderous or… No one cares if you say 'Sarah Jessica Parker.'"

"Probably came to mind because I love *Sex and the City* so much."

"Yes. Everyone knows."

"I'm okay saying how much I love it?"

"I think you're fine."

"It was..." Gnosis put his hand on the window and choked back his tears. "One of my finest creations."

"Treading into dangerous waters now."

"I'm only saying how—"

"That's not all you're saying. Maybe stop."

"But it *was* one of my finest creations!"

"Please stop."

"It developed a tactical advantage we enjoy to this day!"

"Okay," Madelyne conceded, rubbing her temples. "But maybe that's why heavyweights like Sarah are coming out of the woodwork now. Maybe that's why the Twin Chickens awoke earlier than expected. We step our game up, they step up theirs. Before we know it, your finest creation will have a reboot that tries to, I don't know, undo all the damage it caused before."

"Yes!" Hip Gnosis cried, and clapped his hands together. "Hitting the proverbial nail on the proverbial head! That's why it's the proverbial time..." He rubbed his palms together.

"For... ?"

"For us to... I know you don't like the surround-sound voice," Gnosis said. "But you gotta... please?"

Madelyne covered her ears. "Go ahead."

Hip Gnosis boomed, "TIME FOR US TO INITIATE THE NIRVANA PROTOCOL!!!"

Madelyne dropped her hands. "Wait, what?"

"TIME FOR—"

"Stop! I heard you. Are you really prepared to follow through with that level of escalation and everything, *everything*, it will entail?"

"Shit to the yeah," Gnosis replied in his normal voice. "The Twin Chickens have awoken. No more risk-averse counterproliferation."

"Are we even ready?"

Gnosis shrugged. "There won't be a better time than now. The Target will be in the Twin Chickens' area giving the keynote address at a Spiritually Uplifting Communal and Destiny Intensifying Conference at their city's waterfront park"—he held up an index and middle finger—"in two days. We can martyr the Target right in the Twin Chickens' hometown."

Madelyne let out a shaky breath. "I'll issue the orders. Should I call in... ?"

"Yes," Gnosis said grimly. "Call in the Executive Board." Then he put his hands on his hips. "Now... I still think the best episode was season two, episode seven, when Miranda's friend..."

***

"Oh my god!" Joy squealed. "We're in a wormhole!"

"We're in my bathroom," said Jake. "With the lights off. And the door closed."

"But it's—"

"And two strange strangers."

"But it's pitch-black!" said Joy.

"There are no windows."

"Guys," said Ponth, "we're in the wormhole."

"We're in my bathroom. I still smell the result of my morning constitutional."

"Ew," Joy said. "I smell it too."

"Relax, Chickens," Ponth explained. "These things don't go like the movies. You're not gonna see stars and rings of strobing lights."

"If you feel dizzy, sit down," said Sarah.

"I am dizzy," Jake said. "I haven't eaten in days."

"That's not why you're dizzy," Sarah said.

"That's exactly why I'm dizzy."

"Just sit."

"Hey," Jake raised his voice. "I'm not your dog to bark commands at."

Joy sought his arm in the dark and gripped it. "Calm down."

"No." Jake tensed. "I asked for an explanation as to what's going on and now we're standing in my bathroom? Fuck this, I'll figure it out myself."

Sarah's voice resounded, "And how's that been working out for you, Jake Chicken? Figuring it out yourself?"

"Yeah, you know what? We're done. Get out of my house."

"Stop," Joy pleaded.

"Let me go." Jake wriggled out of her grip. "Everyone. Out."

"We're not in your bathroom, Jake," Ponth said.

"Then why's my hand on the doorknob?"

"You open that door," Ponth said, "you're gonna hurt yourself."

"Let hangry man do what he wants," said Sarah, "if that's the only way he'll learn."

Jake opened his bathroom door. "All of you get out of my—"

His knees buckled and his left hip and shoulder slammed into what he assumed was the floor. Then he felt Joy's feathered hands cradling his head. He heard her voice, muffled, say, "So stubborn." Then he took a breath and exhaled.

He felt Joy's feathers on his face and smelled the odor of his bathroom. But the scent had changed slightly, and it now smelled more like a barn. Or a zoo.

And that's when he saw the donkey.

The donkey—gray with a white snout and underbelly—absent-mindedly chewed its cud in the darkness, flicked its tail, turned its head toward Jake, and said, "Yeah, Eeyore."

Jake looked around for Joy but couldn't see her, though he still felt her holding his head. He tried to talk. He wanted to say something along the lines of "are you seeing this shit?" but he couldn't get the words out.

"Yes," he heard Joy's muffled voice say. "I see it! Do you see the lamb?"

Everything for Jake went red. Then orange. Then yellow. Then green, blue, and indigo. Then violet. Then he saw the lamb. Its fleece was not quite as white as snow, but it was white. Perhaps as white as the days-old snow on the concrete streets, laid by that blizzard in '93—the one that came when it was supposed to be spring and he and Raschid looked out the window and Raschid said "Dag. Looks like the nuclear winter of the apocalypse. You think it's the End of Days?" And Jake said… but Jake didn't want to think about that.

He didn't want to think about Raschid. So he focused on the lamb, focused on it so intently he could make out the pink in its ears, one of which the lamb twitched as it laid its body down and rocked side to side.

"It's so stupidly adorable," Jake said, watching the lamb shift left to right, right to left.

".ylgu s'ti etuc os s'tI" .delggig yoJ "?thgiR"
".eroyeE ,haeY" .deyarb dna bmal eht tsap deklaw yeknod ehT
.thgil etihw fo hsalf a saw ereht dna taelb a tuo tel bmal eht ndA

Then Jake's whole body spasmed as he fought the sensation of falling. He began to sob. "It's okay," he could hear Joy soothe, still cradling his head. He blinked and saw her face now, upside-down and hovering over his. She really was so pretty. She wiped his cheeks with her feathers and smiled. "Why are you crying?"

"Get up," Jake whispered, and closed his eyes. "Get up, big head, stop playing."

"Jake?"

"Stupid, big head," he said, laughing nervously. "Come on yo, you play too much." Then he let out a long, pained wail, like a wolf howling at a moon that wasn't there.

He jerked his body again and snapped open his eyes. Joy's nose was pressed against his cheek, her arms and legs wrapped tightly around him. She was surprisingly strong.

"You're hurting me," he said calmly. She released him and they both sat up. Ponth and Sarah came into view. Joy smiled a sad smile and touched a feathered palm to his face. Ponth squatted beside them, watching with concern. Sarah remained standing, giving Jake a knowing look and offering her hand. "On your feet," she said gently. He took her hand, and she pulled him up. Joy and Ponth stood as well. Sarah put her left hand on Jake's shoulder, her right on Joy's.

"I'm sorry," she said to Jake. "I didn't mean to bark commands at you. Or treat you like a child." She looked at both of them. "You two have been through a lot. Everyone knew when the Twin Chickens finally arrived, they'd be broken. They'd have to be. The only people who can save the world are the broken ones." She looked at Jake. "If I tell you to do something, it's not because I'm belittling you. It's because I'm doing everything in my power to protect you, so you can carry on and do what you were put in this world to do."

Jake looked up at Sarah. He was nearly six feet tall and still she towered over him. She gave his shoulder a squeeze, and he saw in her features her absolute sincerity. He nodded respectfully. "Copy," he said. "But can we please get a full brief on what it is you think me and Joy were…" He made air quotes with his fingers. "Put in this world to do."

Sarah let the Chickens go and chuckled. "Is he always this serious?" she said to Joy.

Joy rolled her eyes. "I've been trying."

"Good luck with that," Sarah said.

"Come on," said Ponth. "Full brief with Levi, coming right up."

Ponth stepped forward in the darkness. The rest followed. Joy looked around in the shadows. The smell of Jake's bathroom seemed to take on a humid, stagnant odor. Then her eyes adjusted, and she realized they were, in fact, not in Jake's apartment. They were in a dimly lit, spacious area—like a ballroom—at the front of which was a huge viewing window, at least twenty feet tall by sixty feet wide. Behind this window was what had to be at least six million gallons of murky blue water. Three figures emerged from the shadows and stepped before the window, their blurred silhouettes framed by the gradation of watery blue behind them.

Jake tensed. Joy smiled. "Oh, hi!" she exclaimed.

"Hi," one of the figures replied, and rolled toward them. As the figure came closer, Jake and Joy saw he was a young man in a wheelchair, no older than twenty.

"I'm Joy." She beamed and held out her hand. "Are you Levi?"

The young man shook her hand and smiled. "Yes and no."

"Hey team," Ponth called out to the other two figures. "Don't be shy."

The other two approached. Ponth gestured toward Jake and Joy. "These are the Twin Chickens." Then he pointed a thumb at Levi (not-Levi) and his two companions. "And these," Ponth said, "these are the Worldview Freedom Fighters."

The WVFF cautiously greeted the Twin Chickens. Jake processed his surroundings. "I know this place," he said. "This used to be an aquarium."

"It was abandoned," said Ponth. "Now it's our HQ. So, please, no ego attacks. We got away with your little temper tantrum back there 'cause we were still in the wormhole."

Jake looked at Sarah apologetically. She mouthed the words *it's okay*.

Then Joy patted his shoulder. "What— " Jake began to ask, and she pointed at the huge viewing window. Levi (not-Levi) slumped further in his wheelchair. His eyes rolled back in his head, and he made a series of clicking noises with his throat.

Jake and Joy watched a shadowy, flickering dot in the murky blue rapidly enlarge and solidify in mass and shape as it careened toward the other side of the window and became a behemoth. The Twin Chickens stood agape. It was a whale. And it turned its peculiar snow-white, wrinkled forehead to the side so its left eye pointed directly at its audience.

Joy gripped Jake's arm and laughed. "Thar she blows!"

The glass of the viewing window vibrated as the whale let loose a snort.

"You may not want to joke like that." Levi-not-Levi snapped back to attention. "He's got PTSD too."

"Oh." Joy meekly waved toward the eye of the whale. "I'm so sorry."

"Wait, wait," Levi-not-Levi said as his eyes rolled back into his head. "Nope. You're good. He says that *was* kind of funny."

The whale let loose a series of clicks. The young man in the wheelchair smiled. "He says hi, his name is Leviathan. But his friends call him Levi."

AND NOW...
A DIGRESSION

(Ain't it more of a REGRESSION?)

A regressive digression?
(But it will push things forward, right?)
A PROGRESSIVE REGRESSIVE DIGRESSION!!

(Surprisingly aggressive...)
TRANSGRESSIVE!!

CHAPTER 6

On Monday, August 19th, 1991, at approximately 7:23 p.m. Pacific Standard Time, twenty-one-year-old Alegría Luz Urizar stepped into the aptly named City of Books and immediately wished the air conditioner had not been on so high. It was eighty-three degrees Fahrenheit outside. The sun was out in full strength and would not set for another two hours. It was perfect. And Alegría fought the urge to step back outdoors and continue roaming the streets she had only just then realized were arranged in alphabetical order: Flanders, Everett, Davis, Couch (pronounced "Cooch," apparently), and now her present location, Burnside, upon which was planted this legendarily vaunted and venerable City of Books.

Alegría shivered. Consistent with the weather, she wore only a thin T-shirt beneath her denim overalls. But it was not only the air conditioning giving her the chills. It was the realization. The realization that came as she slid across the smooth concrete floor and looked up at the twenty-foot, wood-beamed ceiling, then back down to the rows and rows and further rows of immaculately shelved books. The realization she had dreamt of this place. Yes, when she was a little girl, huddled in that little corner beneath the unused Concha Acustica in El Parque Municipal de Tecpán. Huddled and teaching herself to read in that little concrete corner that, for her, was Eternity. And when her little eyes closed and she dozed, that little space quite literally became Eternity, and she found herself transported to a concrete city with more books than she could ever read. More stories than she could ever imagine.

Tears rolled down her cheeks, and she put her hand on her belly and stood between two tall rows. She sighed in amused frustration as she cocked her head and scanned the shelved books' spines. This magical city was not a fantasy. It was not a dream. It was very real. All these books were here. They were really here.

And she couldn't understand a single word.

Alegría stroked her belly and whispered, "Supongo que mi sueño no era para mí. Fue para ti. Entenderás *todo*, mi amor. Aprenderé lo que pueda para poder enseñarte."

"Find everything you're looking for?" a halting male voice said behind her.

She spun to find a young man her age, his emaciated body slumped in a wheelchair. He smiled. Alegría smiled back. "Sí… yes, I… yes."

The young man rolled past her. "Let me know if you need help."

"Okay," Alegría said. "Yes. Help. Please."

The young man stopped and turned to face her. "What kind of book are you looking for?"

Alegría mouthed the word *looking* to herself, equated it with *buscar*, then responded, "Yo quiero… big." Her voice grew raspy with desire. "Book. Has everything. Has all the world."

The young man narrowed his eyes, considering. Then he nodded and beckoned with a rail-thin arm. "Follow me."

So she did. Into a small elevator. Up one flight. Out onto the second floor that had more bookshelves than the first. Alegría chuckled, still amazed she was in this place. The young man led her to a back wall, stocked with books Alegría scanned and quickly realized she could understand just fine. They had books in other languages here too. The young man pulled a particularly voluminous tome and held it out.

Alegría smirked. "I read before."

His arm trembled, and he lowered the book to his lap. "You read this already?"

"Three times. Four."

"Wow. What's your favorite part?"

"Como?"

"Your favorite… the best part. The part of the book you enjoyed the most."

"Best?"

"Yes."

"Parte. Of this book?"

"Yes."

Alegría raised her eyes toward the wood-beamed ceiling in thought. The young man waited. He expected her to say something like "the adventure of the windmills" or "the story of Lothario." But Alegría brought her dark eyes down to meet his and said, "I am mad."

"Why are you mad?"

"Don Quixote nunca encuentra a los encantadores."

The young man struggled to recall his high-school Spanish. "He never… los encant… oh, the enchant… He never found the Enchanters!"

Alegría smiled.

"But was he looking for the Enchanters?"

Alegría's face turned dark. "I am. In English."

The young man let out a breath, taken aback. He was starting to understand the gravity of her mission. "You want a big book, like this one. With everything in it. But in English."

Alegría shook her head. "In *American* English."

The young man leaned back in his wheelchair. "Are you ready to do that?"

She bore her eyes into his and grinned a wild grin. And the young man truly did see a madness in her features. A madness with which he was well acquainted. For it was the madness of one who has set forth to accomplish something far beyond their current capabilities.

He beckoned again and rolled away. Alegría followed, navigating the rows of towering shelves. He stopped, pulled a book off a shelf, and handed it to her.

She sounded out the title. "Mo. Bee…" She furrowed her brow. She'd grown to hate the following word after hearing the Monster use it so much.

The young man noticed. "It's no, it's no mal palabra."

Alegría chuckled. His Spanish was terrible. But the young man remained intent on communication. "The uh… can't remember…" He made the motion with a gnarled finger of inserting a key into a keyhole.

Alegría said, with mischief in her eyes, "¿Me vas a enseñar otra mala palabra?"

"Otra... no!" The young man stammered. "I'm trying to... I can't remember the word. The key. The key de la puerta."

"Llave?"

"Llave, that's it."

"Key. I know key."

"Okay, the key." He rolled forward and touched the book in Alegría's hands. "Is to first, primero, read chapter forty-two. That is the key to this book."

"Forty-two?"

"Yes."

"¿Por qué?"

"Porque, hay, the chapter... in books like this, algunas veces, hay una, a chapter, maybe two, that helps you understand, comprender... what the rest of the book is all about."

Alegría nodded and thumbed through the pages.

"Página two-oh-four," the man said.

Alegría flipped to the page and sounded out the words. "Chapter. Forty. Two. The. Witness..."

"Whiteness."

"White. Ness? Como... white?"

"Exactly."

"Como, the page is white."

"Yes and no."

Alegría's eyes impetuously demanded further explanation.

"Yes," the young man said. "Like the page is white. Pero también, como... a person is White."

"Ah! Like you are White."

"Exactly."

"Like I am White."

"But..." the young man stammered again. "You're not White."

Alegría's features grew stormy once more. "I am White."

The young man shifted in his wheelchair. "Well you're... but you're not..."

Alegría cocked her head to the side.

"I don't..." the young man said. "I don't know how to... I don't know the words."

Alegría held up the book. "Does this has the words?"

"I think it tries. Very, very hard."

"How many cost?"

He told her and her face sank, but he had an idea. "I'll hold it for you. Come whenever you want to read it. I am here every day."

She looked at the book. He reached out to take it. "Do you want me to do that? To hold it for you? I won't let anyone else buy it."

"You have trouble to do that?"

He chuckled. "I can't get in trouble for anything here."

She gave him the book. "You help me understand?"

The young man's face lit up. "Por supuesto."

"Claro." Alegría shook her head. "Say 'claro.' Nadie dice 'por supuesto.'"

"Na… no one… says…"

"I help you understand too. With Spanish."

The young man smiled. "Claro," he said.

"Bueno." She nodded and snatched the book back. "We go now."

"Now? Oh… let me… let's go find a seat."

***

It took her four months to work through that chapter. Four months of unpredictable visits, due to, the young man eventually learned, her need to work restaurant shifts whose scheduling she'd often only been informed of that day. But, regardless of what time she'd come, be it minutes after the City of Books opened its doors or minutes before it closed, she'd arrive fully focused and prepared to devote whatever available moments she had to wrestling with the strange American text she swore she'd master.

The issue was Alegría was never satisfied with straightforward translation. When she encountered *Ahab,* she made the young man stop and take her to the Religion section, so she could remind herself where she'd seen that name before. When she encountered *appalled,* she made the young man take her to the Reference section, where she, with great pleasure, discovered that the origin of the word lies in the old French for: "to grow pale." "Germán know this," she asked, "when choose this word?"

"You should have been an etymologist," the young man teased.

"Etamala que?" she said. He laughed and explained. She nodded. Then, Alegría, being Alegría, made them research the etymology of *etymology*. That was how they both learned its Greek root meant "true."

And that was only the first two paragraphs.

"I ask too many questions?" she said at the end of one of their sessions.

The young man shook his head. "Wait until you go back and start reading from the beginning. Don't do it yet. But when you do, I think you'll laugh. Everyone who hasn't read it thinks they know how the book starts." He leaned his head back and proclaimed in a stentorian tone, "*Call. Me. Ishmael.*" He chuckled. "But that's not how it starts."

Alegría then demanded they revisit the Religion section.

This was how they proceeded. Painstakingly. Meticulously. This was how Alegría learned of Pegu, Siam, and Hanover. This was how she learned of the Red Men of America.

"We have Red Men, too, in my town," Alegría shared one visit after she made them peruse the History section. "Kaqchikel. My father no likes them. No likes my best friend, Etelvina, because she Kaqchikel. He likes I no dark like Etelvina. When I am small, my father shows me to all friends, he says 'Look how beautiful. Is so White, like her mother. Es mi pequeña Alegría.'" She took a breath. "She is my little Joy."

The young man listened.

"If I am no White in this country," Alegría said as she sat on a bench in a quiet alcove on the second floor of the bookstore, her wheelchair-bound friend beside her, "am I still Joy?"

The young man brought a quivering hand to his chin and considered how best to respond. Finally, he said, "If I am *not* White…"

"Not White," Alegría repeated.

"Your singular first and third person in the present tense *is* good. If I am not White, am I still Joy? Your past tense *was* not. When I *was* small, my father *showed* me to all his friends. Don't forget your possessive pronouns, *his*... and your subject pronouns... *She* is so White."

Alegría stuck her tongue at him. "*Your* Spanish *was* horrible, too, in past tense. In present, it *is* better."

"Gracias a ti." The young man laughed. "Pero ahora no olvides tus artículos definitivos."

She laughed also. Their dynamic was fresh oxygen to her. There was care. But there was no pity.

The weeks passed. And the young man noticed her belly swell. One day he ventured to ask, "Did the doctor tell you if it's a boy or a girl?"

She beamed. "A girl."

"Have you decided on a name?"

"I will call her Ishmael."

He chuckled. "That's a boy's name."

"Says you," she retorted with a recently acquired idiom.

"Are you and your... husband. Are you excited?"

Alegría returned to the text and read aloud, "The black bisons of distant Oregon." She watched the autumn rain strike the outside of the large window before them. "That is where we are," she mused. "Oregon."

The young man chose not to press any further.

***

"*Wonder ye then,*" Alegría roared one day, "*at the fiery hunt?*"

She laughed, almost maniacally, and the young man laughed with her. His supervisor, a gentle middle-aged man with a salt-and-pepper beard, walked by their bench, checking on the commotion. "This is a respectable establishment," the supervisor said. "You two are not allowed to have this much fun."

Alegría clammed up, not getting the joke. "Sorry, sir."

The supervisor smiled and walked away, not getting that she was not getting his joke.

"He was kidding," the young man said.

"Are you sure?"

"No one's in trouble. Listen..."

"Yes?"

"We finished the chapter. What do you want to do now?"

"Throw this book away and never look at it again."

The young man searched her face.

"I am kidding now," she said. "Now, we need to start with chapter one."

"So listen," he said. "How would you feel about working here?"

"¿Como, un trabajo?"

"Si. Un turno estará disponible."

"When?"

"Soon."

"What would I have to do?"

"Help customers find what they're looking for. Organize the inventory. Work the register. If you work at a restaurant, you can do this. The hardest part of the job is learning where everything is, where all the different sections are." The young man smiled. "But you know all that already."

"My English…"

"Is incredible. And getting better every day. It's amazing how fast you learn everything, it's… you're like, a-a linguistic genius or, you're… amazing."

She looked down. "I don't know."

"When it's quiet," the young man said, "you can explore and read everything and anything you want."

"I don't know if… I'm not… I don't have…"

The young man guessed what she was trying to say. "Do you have an ID? A driver's license?"

"Yes."

"Then you're fine, Alegría. No one cares if you're legal or not. I talked to my boss about it. He agreed with everything. You'd be great here."

"I need to… I need to figure everything out."

"Take your time," he said. "When the shift opens up, it's yours. If you want it."

***

What the young man did not know was there was a Monster

and the Monster had returned. This change in circumstances kept Alegría from visiting her friend at the bookstore for a month. During this month, however, she generated a plot and arrived at a decision. She would take the job, because she wanted it. She would tell the young man she loved him, because she did. And she would make a new home with him. They would live together and work together and raise Ishmael in a world of language and culture and learning and books. People would stare at them, Alegría knew this. She knew that she was beautiful and that the young man was warped and gnarled and stricken with tremors. But he was kind and gentle and patient and smart. He, too, was beautiful. And as his wife, she would be his mirror. She would reflect his beauty to the world. And his patience and intelligence would reflect hers. They would be a family.

This would be her escape from the Monster.

***

As such, approximately five months after she first entered the City of Books, Alegría Luz Urizar, unequivocally swollen with child and soaking wet from the cold winter rain, once more walked into the store and immediately sought out her friend. She did not search for long. On the way to the stairs that led to the second floor where she customarily found the young man, there was an information desk manned by the gentle salt-and-pepper-bearded supervisor. "Hello," he softly said upon her approach, and stood.

"Greetings," she said, more singing than speaking. "Whenceforth gone my sophisticated chum?"

"Please." The supervisor pointed to his chair. "Have a seat."

"I'm okay." She strained her words out of her throat. She could tell something was wrong.

"Please," the supervisor said again. "You're pregnant, and I think… please. Please sit."

Alegría acquiesced. The supervisor rambled about how the young man would do shen muscular this trophy. Alegría did not understand what this shen muscular activity was, but if the young man received a trophy for his efforts, well, that was great.

"Where is he?" she asked.

The supervisor took a breath. "Most young men with Duchenne Muscular Dystrophy don't live as long as he did. We were all surprised, we thought he was going to leave us months ago. We all think... we all know, he hung on a bit longer because of... his friendship. With you."

Alegría's eyes grew hot. "Where is he?"

The supervisor took her hand in his. "He passed away last week."

This was the first time Alegría had confronted this idiomatic euphemism. The cavern in her chest and the swelling in her throat immediately translated its meaning with complete accuracy. But her mind, seeking a loophole or a buttress for denial in the guise of ensuring an absence of miscommunication, linked a series of words that tumbled down the back of her throat. She made an odd gargling sound, shuffling and shifting those words with her tongue and breaking them between her teeth. They were the same words she had spoken those fifteen years ago when she was first brought to her mother's grave after the earthquake—she just needed to alter the subject pronoun and say them in English, which she did with an unblinking smile. "When will he come back?"

The supervisor squeezed her hand, realizing he needed to speak with complete pellucidity. "He died," he said, bracing himself against his own expression. "He is dead."

Alegría pulled her hand away and brought it to her mouth. Her palm covered her lips and her forefinger blocked her nostrils, increasing the sound of rushing air as her breath forced past this obstruction.

"He spoke to me about, before..." the supervisor stammered. "He, before, he said he had spoken with you also. The job. About the job. I have been holding off on posting, on hiring anyone for the job. For his job. We need to hire someone new. I hoped we would see you again. If you would like the job, his job, working here. We would love it if you joined us."

Alegría removed her hand from her mouth, arched her back slightly to lean her belly forward, and stood. Without a word, she turned and ambled toward, then up, the stairs that led to the second floor. She grazed her fingers against the wood of the shelves with which she was now wondrously familiar and made her way over to the Literature section. Mann... McCarthy... Milton... nope, too far... here... Melville.

She pulled the dense tome from its position. Flipped past the table of contents. Read out loud the first word of Moby-Dick.

"Etamala que," she said with a whispered giggle, confident the young man would have appreciated the joke...

And that was when her water broke.

CHAPTER 7

On Monday, August 19th, 1991, at approximately 4:23 p.m. Eastern Standard Time, thirty-one-year-old Miriam Rabinowitz shivered from the full-blast air conditioning in the Museum of Modern Art; stood before a slender, black, six-foot, ten-inch oil painting; and smiled. The nine-year-old boy beside her fidgeted and said, "There's nothing there."

"Yakov," she said patiently. "Everything is there."

"It's just all black," said the boy.

"It's not just all black."

"It is."

"It's not." She bent a little to address him at eye level. "Look at it. Really look at it. What do you see?"

The boy faced the painting. "It's black and dark brown and more black, and there's a black line in the middle, so the middle's like blackety-black black black."

She fixed the collar of his thin blue polyester windbreaker. "What else?"

The boy stepped forward and squinted and read out loud the title card, "Abraham." He stepped back and leaned his body against hers. "Mom, I don't get it."

Miriam laughed and grabbed his hand. The boy squirmed, but she gripped tighter. "Stop laughing at me," he said.

"My lamb." Her face grew serious. "I would never laugh at you. Now straighten up, please."

He did so. Straight as a board, awaiting further instruction. He'd make a good soldier. And though Miriam enjoyed this obedient disposition, it was a trait that caused her concern. Her husband broached the idea once of sending him to grow up in Israel. She shot that down immediately. He'd be compelled into military service there. And of the many things for which she prayed, her son never having to know war was among her top priorities.

"You could not try so hard to get it," she said. "You could try to relax and let it in."

The boy faced the painting again. Stared at it. Breathed. "It makes me think of Dad."

Miriam released his hand and grazed her fingers along the soft little hairs on the nape of his neck. "And there you are," she said. "You get it perfectly."

The boy leaned back into his mother. She bent again and kissed the crown of his head.

***

Hours later, at approximately 9:36 p.m., Miriam exited the Utica Avenue subway station at Eastern Parkway with her son and instantly knew something was wrong. The surrounding gusts of wind were blowing at a good nine miles per hour. She could smell the rage they carried. A familiar smell, mixed with the odor of marijuana and evaporated stout—which was how it often smelled on those balmy heat-wave nights. But tonight was not one of those nights. Hurricane Bob had just torn through the eastern shore of Long Island and assailed its way toward New England. Its passing effect on Brooklyn, however, was pleasant and peripheral. A light rain had finished some hours before, and the air had been cooled to a perfect seventy-five degrees. On nights like this, everything usually did not smell like smoked and spilled frustrations. On nights like this, everything usually felt calm.

Miriam's ears perked and strained and focused, seeking data that could confirm or deny what her olfactory and enteric nerves had already surmised. She clutched Yakov's hand and pulled him south down Utica, through the crowd that would ordinarily still be shopping at the Jewish-run pharmacy, the Korean produce store, the pawn shop, the donut shop, the pizza shop, the West Indian fish and chicken restaurant, the African hair braiding salon, the cake bakery, the menswear outlet, the deli, the optometrist, the CTown, the 99-cents store—then she heard it. The resounding first bits of corroborating information. But no, she thought, instinctively avoiding the oblique glances of the crowd, no, those were not gunshots. Likely, those were the retorts of a car's backfiring exhaust. But when she and Yakov crossed the intersection at Union, continuing south, Miriam realized most of the businesses had pulled down their overhead security gates. No one was shopping. No one was waiting at the bus stop for the B46. Breaking glass and shouted chants echoed, increasing in volume and clarity. Miriam discerned the words a mob a block ahead roared. She froze.

Miriam's grandmother, hearing things no one else could hear, had lived her final years folded in a corner of Miriam's parents' living room. The woman refused to leave that corner, let alone that house, and everyone always said that in both body and spirit, Miriam was the spitting image of this broken matriarch. As such, Miriam always worried she would one day begin to hear things too. So, she couldn't help but sardonically realize, once she determined what the crowd ahead was chanting, how she now fervently prayed she was, in fact, hearing things. She looked to her son for assurance. The boy, reading his mother's face, forced himself to control his breathing. He stated calmly, "They're saying 'the Jews killed the kids.'"

Miriam thought of Oregon. She didn't know why, she'd never been there, she'd only read about it in books. Books like, oh yes, Moby-Dick. She loved Moby-Dick. She'd tried to no avail to get Yakov to read a highly abridged children's version, but the boy had not inherited her deep affinity for stories. He was more like his father, with a good head for numbers and a tendency to cut straight to the point in both thought and communication. What was it Melville had said? About the black bisons of distant Oregon? About the instinct of the knowledge of the demonism in the world? The crowd ahead screamed. Then what sounded like a hailstorm startled her. She looked wildly about. Seeking a place for refuge, escape, mercy, or deliverance. From the buildings ahead, debris showered onto the cars below—pipes, bricks, old electronics. An acrid stench filled the air. Miriam's right arm jerked so hard it hurt her neck. Yakov had tugged at it with all his strength. "Mom," he said with a calm that frightened her. How could he be so calm? But had not Dawid, the boy-hero, had he not also been calm when he faced down the giant of…

"Mom. We need to get home."

"We have to run, we have to—"

"Home is right there." The boy pointed south toward President Street. "It's right around the corner."

Yakov pulled her onward and Miriam dutifully followed. But within a few steps, a glass bottle shattered at her feet. She let out a cry. Three teenagers appeared, one of whom gestured west and barked, "Fuck back to Kingston where you from."

Miriam could not tell if the teenagers were communicating a threat or suggesting a more beneficial course of action. Yakov seemed not to care. He stooped and grabbed a shard of broken glass. The teens narrowed their eyes. Yakov pointed south. "We live there."

"There?" A teen spoke. Yakov nodded. Miriam noticed an overturned car down the street. It had been lit aflame. That's where the acrid smell was coming from. Yakov grabbed his mother's hand and said again, "We live there."

The teens looked from boy to mother and back. "A'ight," one said. "Lead the way."

Yakov used both hands to gesture to either side of Miriam. Then he touched his own back and positioned himself directly in front of his mother. The teens followed his wordless commands. Two flanked Miriam's left and right and the third stood at her rear, forming a small phalanx around her which, through the screams, smoke, sprinting rioters, and woefully outnumbered police, pushed forward, led by her son, her Yakov, her lamb, her lion, her stolid little Maccabee.

The phalanx approached the corner at President Street, and a blue-donned cop jumped out of his car and shouted something unintelligible before being rushed and tackled to the ground by another man. The amorphous crowd thickened and shifted its chant to a clear monosyllable: "Jews! Jews! Jews!" Miriam's eyes followed the trajectory of a small television set arcing from the roof of a four-story building and landing on a police car below. Then the attack came. The left side of Miriam's head smarted from the impact with the shoulder of the teenager at her side. The protector on her left flank shoved back against whatever force had risen from the depths of Sheol while Yakov continued to pull her forward. The phalanx tightened. There were claws trying to reach past the phalanx and grab her hair. And there were words, so many words that Miriam would fight to forget all the rest of her days.

"West," Yakov shouted above the din when they reached the corner, and the phalanx followed, banking right. How were his cardinal directions so accurate? He always seemed to know exactly where he was and where he was going. A few weeks ago, during an excursion in Prospect Park, he and Miriam had chosen to wander the surrounding forest after leaving the zoo, and Miriam subsequently lost her way. Yakov peered at the sunlight slipping through the thick oak leaves, muttered "that's east," then led them back to the park's main road. The phalanx passed the graffiti-tagged rolled-down metal gate of the corner shop and went through the swarm of the surrounding crowd, some of whom still lobbed curses and spittle and vehement glares. Miriam saw a station wagon on the sidewalk, against the wall of her apartment building, on the right side of its entrance. The phalanx pushed through the crowd. The steel bumper of the station wagon was partially torn from its fascia, the center of its hood crumpled upward like a small tent. The crowd blocking the entrance stared at Miriam. "Let them through," the teenager at her right commanded. "They live here." There was a response of wild and varied murmurings. Then Miriam heard a man scream her name.

She turned to see her husband sprinting toward her from across the street. She opened her mouth to shout his name back, but he was so fast, he'd reached her and shoved through the crowd and the phalanx and wrapped his right arm around her and picked up his son with his left, shouting "She's my wife. We live here," before she barely got out the first syllable: "Jah."

They rushed through the entrance, into the initial enclave of their apartment building, and Joshua put Yakov down and fumbled with his keys so he could open a second door. Yakov stepped toward the three teens who now stood at the main entrance, blocking it so no one could follow the family in. Yakov traded words with the three guardians, though Miriam could not make out those words over the roar of the mob outside. Joshua opened the second door and beckoned his family through. He saw one teenager touch the top of his son's head and his fists clenched. "They helped us," Miriam said. "All down the street they helped us get home." Joshua relaxed. Yakov went back to his father. Joshua picked him up again. The family walked through the door. "We should invite them in," Yakov whispered in his father's ear. Joshua turned, keeping the door open with his foot to face the three guardians, but they were gone.

The family walked across the lobby and up a stairwell, and Miriam, trembling, drew closer beneath her husband's arm. Yakov buried his face into his father's neck, then whispered while they went up the stairs, "They said it's good you invited them in."

Joshua tensed. "I can find them later. They tell you their names?"

Yakov nodded. "Gabe, Big Mike, and… Az… Azruh…" He struggled with the third name. "Azrael."

"Okay," Joshua said, and unlocked their second-floor apartment. They walked into their narrow hallway.

"Why do you want to find them later if—"

"Yakov." Joshua put his son down. "Why are you whispering? Say what you want to say."

"Don't yell at him," said Miriam.

"No one's… I just don't want him getting into this habit of whispering."

"Take off your shoes," Miriam said to the boy, and locked the apartment door. "You want to watch a show?"

"No, hold up," Joshua said, trying to make eye contact with his son who was still gazing toward the door. "Look me in the eye and speak up, please."

Miriam stormed off. The door of the singular bedroom slammed. Yakov stared at his father, and Joshua did not like the look on his son's face.

"I just asked," Yakov spoke up, "why you wanted to find

Mike, and Gabe, and Azrael later."

"That's it?" Joshua asked, annoyed at how his son was staring at him as if he were crazy.

"Yes, sir."

"You sure?"

"Yes, sir," Yakov replied, but he said this as if he were bored and knew the answer to the question already, or no longer cared.

"To thank them. That's all. You okay?"

"Yes." The boy nodded and took off his shoes, smiling to himself.

Joshua removed his shoes as well and walked down the hallway, toward his bedroom, to deal with his angry wife. "Come on, guys," Joshua heard Yakov whisper behind him. "I'll show you my comic books."

A chill went down Joshua's spine. He turned and watched his son go into the living room. He walked back down the hall, stood by the living room entrance, and listened to his son shuffle through the comics he was allowed to keep in a neat stack by the hi-fi music tower in the top right corner of the room. Joshua strained to hear his son's voice, muttering and low.

"You like that one? That one's okay. This one's my favorite. Uh huh. Captain America. He's my favorite."

AND NOW…
(And then?)

Now and then.

(Again and again?)
BACK…

(Forward?)
***BACK…* to the main storyline!!**

CHAPTER 8

The Worldview Freedom Fighters assessed the Twin Chickens with caution. The smallest of the group of three, a female, piped up. "Whoa, whoa, whoa…"

"That's a lot of *whoas*," said Joy.

"So you guys can actually *see* Levi?" asked the female.

"You don't see the fifty-ton mammal?" said Jake. "In the six-million-gallon tank of water?"

"No," the young woman replied. "I don't." Then she put her hand on the shoulder of the wheelchair-bound young man. "Only Levi-not-Levi can hear Levi. That's why we call him Levi-not-Levi, because he's the only one who can communicate with Levi, so for all intents and purposes he *is* Levi, even though he's *not* really Levi, but since Levi talks through Levi-not-Levi, it kind of makes Levi-not-Levi the equivalent of Levi, make sense?"

Jake stared, dumbfounded the young lady had said all that in one breath.

Joy laughed long and hard. "You are so cute!"

"I'm glad you think so." The young woman blushed. "Sorry, I've got a bit of verbal diarrhea, we're all just so incredibly, fabulously, astoundingly—"

"Don't say 'verbal diarrhea,'" said Jake.

"I'm sorry." She clammed up.

"Don't stop talking," Joy said, and shot Jake a look. "He's just afraid. Someone vomited on us earlier and—"

"I'll read vomit," said Jake. "Don't make me read diarrhea."

And at that, the whale let out a click that shook the room. Jake and Joy jumped, startled. Levi-not-Levi let out a "wow." And the third member of the WVFF, quiet until this point, stepped forward and pulled down the hood of their sweatshirt so their face was in full view. "Fuck outta here," they grunted. "You can manifest metaphors? And y'all claim you can see Levi? What's he look like?"

Jake narrowed his eyes. "Why don't you ask Levi-not-Levi?"

"I can't actually see Levi," said Levi-not-Levi.

Jake pointed at the young lady. "She just said—"

"I said he *hears* Levi," said the young woman.

"Hearing isn't even an accurate..." said Levi-not-Levi. "It's more of a sensing, channeling. I know when he's here, but I can't..."

Jake and Joy traded a look. "Well," said Joy, "we see him. Here. Literally."

"So what's he look like?" the hooded member asked again.

"I don't know," said Jake. "Like a big fucking whale." He turned to Joy. "What's he look like to you?"

"Familiar," Joy said, and smiled. "He looks familiar." Then she extended her hand toward the hooded individual. "I'm Joy, by the way."

The hooded member shook her hand. "Azrael."

Jake froze. Azrael stared at him. The young woman said, "And hi and hello and good morrow to you two, my name is Ms. Hai Le, and I like to say *Ms.* before *Hai* because *Hai* is a boy's name, and I'm, a girl, but then people think maybe I'm married and Hai Le is my husband, but I'm not married, I'm not (such sexism) at least not yet anyway (if ever) so mostly these days I try to make it simpler for everyone because, shoot, what's in a name but a series of letters set in a specific permutation, nothing more nothing less, so you can just call me..." She caught her breath and smiled. "Hailee."

Joy observed the young woman closely, and her voice came out as a whisper. "Hi, Hailee."

Sarah tapped her smartphone and said to Ponth, "Nimrod can't make it. Got some things to take care of at the bar."

"Is what it is," Ponth replied. "Alrighty guys, now that everyone's through sniffing each other's butts, I promised the Chickens here some answers."

"You did," said Jake.

"And answers you shall have," Ponth said, and pointed toward the whale. "Ask Levi anything you like."

"Come on," Levi-not-Levi said, and rolled toward the huge viewing window. Jake and Joy followed.

"Yo, don't start yet," Azrael said suddenly. "Wait up one...

hold on." And they pulled Hailee, Ponth, and Sarah aside.

"They ain't ready for this," said Azrael.

"Preaching to the choir," Sarah mumbled.

"Whose choir?" said Ponth. "Not mine. Let them talk to Levi. Give them the chance."

"It's good they can manifest metaphors..." said Azrael.

"We've also seen them enact a time-space compression..." said Ponth.

"That's all gravy, but—"

"... and manipulate quantum stochastic processes."

"We haven't actually seen them do that one," Sarah reminded him.

"I believe them," said Ponth.

"Either way, that's grade-school shit," said Azrael.

"Come on," said Ponth. "It's at least high-school shit."

"Doesn't matter." Azrael pointed a thumb toward the viewing window. "Cause Levi's on that post-PhD fellowship shit. Anything he got to say? It's gonna go way over their heads. Them two Chickens need more time to hatch."

"I agree," said Sarah.

"*You* suggested we bring them here," said Ponth.

"Yes," Sarah admitted. "Then we had the episode in the wormhole."

"The episode in... ?" Azrael asked.

"Little temper tantrum Jake had back—" said Ponth.

"My man," said Azrael. "That is not good."

"What do you suggest then, Azi?" Ponth asked.

"They buzzing with anxieties that can pop off any moment," said Azrael. "Felt it the second they walked up in here. It's dangerous. Take 'em back home. Give 'em more time to heal."

"We don't have more time," said Ponth. "And you know how I work. You see a problem, come up with a solution. So what's your solution?"

"How about an alternative assessment?" Hailee broke in.

"Please," said Ponth.

"They may not understand everything at first," said Hailee. "But I mean, there's so much they can do already. They might understand everything with some subsequent reinforcement. Like an assigned follow-up activity."

"What, like homework?" Azrael laughed. "Might work for Joy. But Jake? Dude's not the good-student type. He the waiting-for-recess type."

"Then we give them a go-out-and-play-type follow-up activity," said Hailee.

"Best training's on-the-job training," Ponth muttered. "That is a solution. I like it."

"What solution?" said Sarah. "What are you thinking?"

"I'll tell you later," Ponth said, and walked away, heading for an exit on the other side of the room. "Let them talk to Levi. That's an order. Let me know how they do."

"Where are you… ?" Sarah asked.

"I'll be back," Ponth said from the shadows that swallowed him whole.

Azrael sucked his teeth and nodded at Levi-not-Levi, who was still beside the viewing window with Jake and Joy. Leviathan the Whale shifted so he could train his right eye, bluish gray and the size of a baseball, directly on the Twin Chickens. Joy touched a feathered palm to the glass. The whale clicked. Levi-not-Levi clicked back, then said, "He says he'll do his best to explain everything in a way you'll understand. Where would you like to start?"

"Start," Joy said, and shot Jake a mischievous grin, "in the beginning."

***

In the ground-level atrium of the main building of HG Inc.'s corporate campus, the worker ants scurried to and fro with a happy hum. Director Gnosis had just shot out a company-wide email with the quarterly results and key metrics report that thanked everyone for their contributions to incremental but indispensable short-range successes and requested that, as a reward, everyone step away from their desks and monitors and cubicles and do absolutely anything except work for the next two hours. Anything. Take a walk, take a nap, watch a movie, hit the gym, anything. Just not work. Most elected to stay indoors (it was raining outside), grab coffee and baked goods from the ground-level café (Director Gnosis said it would be free during this two-hour period), and lounge in the brightly colored modern-style womb chairs spotted throughout the atrium. O happiest of all happies! What more could a group of persons desire? Remember this, you the noble who steps amongst the aggregate humanities: There is no contention that cannot be squelched, no transgression that cannot be vanished, no crime that cannot be forgiven with the disbursement of unexpected paid leave and free lemon-rosemary scones!

And so, the workers, their mouths stuffed with baking powder and wheat chased down by Ecuadorian Arabica with vanilla whipped cream, laughed gently and chatted heartily and discussed their weekend plans.

Then Executive Associate Director Liz Mammon walked into the building.

The workers' hum decreased to a barely audible din. You see, this was a bit of an event; executive leadership was rarely seen. Sure, every employee knew what EAD Mammon looked like, and most partook in the insidious gossip surrounding her—one camp proclaiming she had only risen to her current position of power because of affairs with either one or both of the other two EADs, Tim Belhor and Ari Milcom, both male; the other camp counter-proclaiming that such slander was the result of sedulous sexism and the persistent envy of the idea and ideal of a woman shattering glass, silicone, acrylic, and polycarbonate ceilings to get somewhere, do something, and be someone—but practically not a soul present had met or seen or spoken with the woman in person, let alone the other three members of the Executive Board.

EAD Mammon unbuttoned her gray mélange blazer, looked about, and smiled.

She was surprisingly average looking at first glance. Not a tall woman, but not short. Neither startling, nor bland. The trick was to catch her eyes. They were a blazing green, the stuff of literary trope, and if you held her glance for more than a second, you'd find yourself gaping into an infinite maw. One poor employee did just this, and promptly passed out. He hit the floor. His colleagues rushed to help. EAD Mammon laughed. "I forget I have that effect on people."

Nervous giggles rippled through the crowd, clipped short as three more individuals entered the building. Everyone muttered. Laying eyes on one member of the Executive Board was significant enough. But now all four stood in the hall.

EAD Ari Milcom carried himself as everyone always thought he would: ramrod straight with chest and chin jutting forth like the former military man he was known to have been. Milcom had apparently risen to the rank of general when he served in the service prior to joining HG Inc., but if you asked anyone specifically under which service he served, or over which campaigns he campaigned, you'd likely be met with little more than a blank stare.

EAD Tim Belhor was, in all ways, the polar opposite of Milcom. Short and scrawny with long, sandy, scruffy hair, he wore skateboard shoes with his two-piece suit, no tie, took a long inhale of his designer e-vaporizer, nodded at the crowd, and croaked a laconic "S'up."

Then there was Deputy Director Sam Ekron. They were taller than Milcom and skinnier than Belhor and carried themself with an air of relaxed authority appropriate for the individual who was second-in-command of HG Inc., second only to Director Gnosis himself.

No employee present that day would ever really be able to recall observing the executives subsequently trek up the escalator to the top floor. One instant, they were standing in the atrium, and the next, they were standing at the access-controlled entrance to Director Gnosis's office suite. There had been many different office suites over the years—HG Inc. had, for various reasons pertaining to the improvement of throughput and the strategic need to fully leverage the effects of creeping normality, relocated countless times before. The amount of times every single executive had gathered to be physically present for a direct meeting with the director, however, was astonishingly countable. Before this day, there had only been two…

The first had occurred at a time when things were oddly

simpler yet much more complex. The world around the five of them seemed murkier, more dangerous, and less stable. But in their youth, they felt within themselves a confident solidarity in who they were and what they decided. "Soooo," Hip Gnosis had asked them (though that wasn't his name back then), "how shall we deal with the competition?"

"Crush them," Milcom had said.

"We can't," Belhor had responded with a drag of his joint. "Let's just avoid 'em and do our own thing."

Mammon had pursed her lips. "Though I agree with this doing of our own thing, I don't think that should entail us doing no thing. If we can't take on the competition directly, fine. But we should still work hard to make our entity just as good, if not better, than theirs."

"How?" said Belhor. "Don't know if you noticed, but they've established a bit of a monopoly."

"Then we chip away at their hegemony," said Mammon.

"We'd need more resources before we conduct such a campaign," said Milcom.

"Then we're in a conundrum," said Belhor. "Because we can't gather assets in an environment where the competition runs, you know, everything." He took another drag. "That's why I say, fuck it. Let's just chill."

"What if," said Ekron, quiet until this point, "we were able to establish a foothold in a barely touched emerging market?"

Milcom, Belhor, and Mammon perked up. Hip Gnosis smiled. Ekron was his favorite. This was why.

"And where is this market?" Mammon asked.

"Far," said Ekron. "Very far. It is not convenient in any way, shape, or form. Anyone who tries to get there has a good chance of being erased from existence. Our competitors made entry, but they haven't been doing a good job with follow-through. This place is harsh. Its people are insanely stubborn. But if we move quickly, I think we could take it over."

"Then we could garner our own resources," said Mammon.

"I think so," said Ekron.

"Resources we could use to directly confront our rivals," said Milcom.

"Long-term strategy, yes," said Ekron.

"And if we win, we can finally drop all this bullshit and do whatever we want," said Belhor.

"If we win, sure," said Ekron.

"I dig it," Hip Gnosis spoke up. "What's the first step?"

"We need someone to go out there and start networking," Ekron answered. "One of us needs to go build some bridges."

"Psh," said Hip Gnosis. "Bridges be my middle name."

So building bridges is what Hip Gnosis did. He set out to find this new place, befriending two local warlords on the way, and the warlords agreed to build the first bridge; the one that gave Hip Gnosis access to this new territory. Then he hit the ground running, gathering market intelligence on exactly what the inhabitants of this domain wanted. And what Hip Gnosis found was these inhabitants had no idea what they wanted. Sure, they wanted *something,* but they themselves had not figured out exactly what that something was. It was an odd condition. But it was a beneficial condition, ready and ripe for aggressive exploitation. And so, after some time, Hip Gnosis called a second meeting between himself and his cohort. A meeting in which he provided a presentation on this condition titled:

"The Human Condition," Gnosis began. "A condition of constant *need.* Food, water, air, shelter, sleep, sex, love, and this really weird thing, I don't understand why they need it so bad, they call it, get this, they call it 'creativity.'"

Mammon, Belhor, and Milcom laughed. Ekron remained silent.

"When these guys, for whatever reason, can't meet any of these needs," Gnosis continued, "they either die, or go legitimately insane."

"Sir," Ekron ventured, "all these things you mention, all these needs. Whatever isn't right in front of them, they can easily give each other."

"I knowwww." Hip Gnosis giggled. "But for some reason, *they* don't know that. It's like they're walking around with their eyes closed. So what I've started, and what we have to keep doing, is... we have to keep convincing them all their needs, all of them, can be met by *us*."

Mammon, Belhor, and Milcom hummed in approval. Ekron folded their arms.

"But the operation will need to expand," Hip Gnosis continued. "Assertively. We'll need to utilize all our particular talents to efficiently reorganize our incorporation. Mammon, Belhor, Milcom, I want to put each of you in charge of your own division."

The three nodded in assent. But Ekron spoke up. "With all due respect, I think there are too many factors you're not considering."

"Like?" Hip Gnosis asked.

"The competition. They're not going to stop peddling their own counterinfluence. There are already prophecies floating around. About agents who have yet to appear. Agents who will remind the humans—"

"That's why I like you," Hip Gnosis cut in. "You were never a yes-person. That's why I want you to be my deputy, second only to me, my right hand, in charge of overseeing the strategies of each of the three divisions, ensuring cross-programmatic communication and coordination occurs. What say you, cuz?"

Ekron thought for a moment, then unfolded their arms. "I humbly accept."

Mammon clapped her hands. Milcom raised a fist. Belhor rolled his eyes.

"But," Ekron continued, "that still doesn't resolve what—"

"And my first charge to you, my right hand," said Hip Gnosis, "is… create an influence to counter the countering influence you so wisely mention."

Ekron fought back a smile. "I already did."

Hip Gnosis cocked an eyebrow. "Pray tell."

"It's a long-range, multi-level campaign that would culminate in an endgame I call 'the Nirvana Protocol.' Would you like me to lay it out for you?"

Everyone leaned forward.

"Lay it out for me, Ekron," Hip Gnosis said. "Lay it allllll out."

But that was then. When the world was chaos, and they were simple and strong. As time went on, this reversed. The world became more organized while they became more fluid. They found that in order to maintain their market dominance, they had to be willing to shift, to change, to adapt—so they could keep convincing the customers they remained the answer to their every desire. And now, the four executives of the Board stood before Hip Gnosis's door, as they had done only twice before, all hoping that maybe, just maybe, everything they had been working for was finally coming to fruition.

The door opened and they saw a red-haired woman with no face stand before them.

"Guys!" Hip Gnosis called from inside. "That's my new special assistant, Madelyne. Come on! We got some shit to catch up on! The Nirvana Protocol is going down!"

Madelyne beckoned the four executives, "Please come in."

***

Jake and Joy felt the reverberating clicks of Leviathan the Whale even through the two-foot-thick acrylic viewing window. It felt as if the cetacean's sound was knocking on their bones. Levi-not-Levi pursed his lips, then let loose a beatboxed boom bap in time with the whale's clicks. Azrael swayed and Hailee clapped on the backbeat. Joy giggled. Jake shifted uncomfortably. Sarah watched everyone intently. Levi-not-Levi interpreted what the whale said:

"Begin at beginning, the beginning, the beginning
mm, uh, uh huh, uh huh. Yeah, uh. Uh huh, uh huh…
I got, yeah, uh huh, uh huh… I got, mm, uh huh, uh huh…
I got epochs laid out in a fiery blaze, watch your gaze,
don't get dazed, I only seek to amaze.
And if you ain't picking up on every issue laid out,
just relax, I got stacks, and we can always come back.

You see the Water was the daughter of the Element Prime.
Who told the Water of the Chaos at the beginning of time.

Who told the Water when the Word spoke, 'Let there be light.'
That's when the Chaos made a naos, ceding Shifts left and right.

Now how the Chaos made those lamb shifts a wonder to hold,
was oscillation of a pendulum six hundred years old,
whose first swing shift y'all remember worked during night
at the time of divine narration gathered for sight.

But remember now to never, ever, ever assume,
that these naked singularities are singular boons.
Peekaboo, Waterloo—they tend to coming in twos,
that's why The Story of the Glory paired/appeared with the Boo

DA! Stating in waiting where the creating was true.
YA! Lying, denying about the nature of who
WHA? went and rose strong in the flower of East,
'cause the Sun done shone alone in the tale of the Beast.

Yeahhh, rewriting all the time at the restart of time.
It even whispered to the Mister known as final-in-line.
Kept taking faces off the moons and making old stories null,
leading, needing, feeding myths about the Individual.

So when the next Shift came in the form of the Horde
a systematic automatic influence had now scored,
throwing points for mad murder allll up on the board,
in what was supposed to be a shift toward a Lydian chord."

"*Wait!!!*" Jake suddenly shouted. Levi-not-Levi paused. Everyone looked at Jake, who laughed long and hard, fighting back tears. Joy smiled at him, but with caution. Was he finally letting a profound moment in? He leaned toward her and said intensely, "The subway. You remember?"

"Which part?" she said back.

"The 'Yeah, Eeyore' part."

"Yes. You are Eeyore."

"He said *we* were Eeyore."

"I am not Eeyore."

"He said that's what we are."

"I don't want to be an Eeyore."

"He didn't say we were Eeyore."

Joy flapped her wings. "You just said he said we were!"

Jake laughed. And though frustrated, Joy couldn't help but laugh with him. She enjoyed seeing him like this. This must have been what he looked like when he was a little boy.

"Yeah, Eeyore the donkey and the lamb," Jake rambled. "The donkey, the donkey, remember what you said, he didn't say 'Yeah! Eeyore!' That's what *you* said, *he* said that's what, what *we* are, but he didn't, I don't think he thought you were thinking 'Yeah, Eeyore'."

"What did he think I was thinking?"

"What the Whale just said about what the Word spoke."

"Let there... ?" Joy ventured.

Jake nodded vigorously. "He thought you were thinking..." He laughed again. "He didn't think you said *yeah, Eeyore,* he thought you said *yehi 'or.*"

Joy cocked her head in confusion.

"*Yehi 'or.* It's Hebrew," Jake explained. "For 'let there be light.'"

Joy's eyes widened and a fifteen-watt clear glass light bulb materialized and hovered over her and Jake's heads. It lit up the cavernous atrium.

"Oh my—" Hailee said, and shielded her eyes. The whale clicked. "He said that's impressive." Levi-not-Levi laughed. Azrael barely blinked. And Sarah asked, "Guys, who is this *he* you're talking about?"

But before the Twin Chickens could answer, the voice of Ponth J. Sahib echoed through the atrium. "Alright, kiddies," he said as he appeared holding a pizza box, "let's skedaddle."

Sarah furrowed her brow. "Where did you—"

"Hold this please?" Ponth handed her the pizza and pulled out his smartphone. He tapped and swiped at its screen, and it said, "Please state your full name to complete author—"

"Ponth J. Sahib." He beckoned to Jake and Joy, then headed

for the double-doored exit.

"But we just got here!" Joy protested.

"What's the rush?" asked Jake.

"Bit of a time crunch I can explain in a few," Ponth answered. "Come on."

Sarah and the Twin Chickens grudgingly followed.

"Enchanting to meet you all!" Joy waved to the Worldview Freedom Fighters on their way out. Azrael nodded with a forced smile. Hailee beamed. "Charming! Truly! We cannot wait to see you both at some—"

"Let's go," Ponth said. "Wormhole's gonna close."

"Bye, Levi-not-Levi." Joy smiled sweetly at the young man. He smiled back.

Jake waved awkwardly at the whale. "See ya around?"

The whale winked.

"Five seconds," Ponth said.

The Worldview Freedom Fighters watched the Twin Chickens follow Ponth and Sarah through the exit doors.

"Wow," Hailee said breathlessly. "They... they're amazing."

"They're okay," Azrael said.

"But, the light bulb..." said Hailee.

"They got talent," Azrael conceded. "But outta all the knowledge Levi just dropped, all they picked up was a little fraction of what was in the first couplet."

The whale clicked. Levi-not-Levi heavily sighed. "Did he say something?" Hailee asked.

"He said we can always go back," Levi-not-Levi responded.

"Ain't got time for that," Azrael said. "Them Twin Chickens don't get their shit together? We're fucked."

CHAPTER 9

Jake leaned over his kitchen sink and dry heaved. The second wormhole journey, unaccompanied as it was by further apparitions involving barnyard animals' semiotic representation of sacred and/or scientific utterance, was even more physically unpleasant than the first. Jake was not a vomiter. He took pride in the strength of his gastrointestinal system. Even when they had forced his platoon to drink all that water—to drink and drink until he felt the dissolution of the boundary between skull and open air; to drink and drink until his fellow plebeians succumbed to the onset of hyponatremia and spasmed and regurgitated the force-fed ideas of themselves onto the dehydrated tufts of grass—even then, Jake did not vomit.

"Who's *they*?" Joy asked as she rubbed his upper back.

Jake perched the sharps of his elbows on the edge, where aluminum met ceramic, then perched his chin on the heels of his hands and thought about the *they*. There was always a *they*; an all ways, everywhere *them* of which Jake had never not been aware, even when their every then and their every now danced and flitted on the outskirts of his peripheral vision. Even when they shifted their who and solidified their what and banged the brims of their stiff-brimmed campaign hats and laughed or grinned or sinned with their eyes. *I think you're still dehydrated one-two-six, I think you need another bottle of this H-two-oh…*

"I'm here," Joy said, and wrapped her arms around Jake's waist and squeezed. For he was shivering even though the basement apartment was a perfect room-temperature seventy-five degrees Fahrenheit. "Come back."

Jake opened his eyes and took a slow breath. One, two, three, four. Hold. One, two, three, four. Exhale. One, two…

Joy smiled. "You did better this time."

Jake smiled back.

"And you didn't freak out when I read your thoughts," she said.

"Getting used to you, I guess."

Joy crinkled her nose and softly tapped her head against his shoulder.

"They need to eat," Sarah said to Ponth as they watched the Twin Chickens while standing in the living room.

Ponth took the pizza box from her. "That's what this bad boy's for." He placed the box on Jake's coffee table. "Come on guys, dig in."

The Twin Chickens approached the pizza as if it might sprout legs and run away. "The way things have been going," Joy said, "it might do that." Jake nodded and as they reached the pizza, he fell to his knees before it and said with great emotion:

בָּרוּךְ אַתָּה ה', אֱ-לֹהֵינוּ מֶלֶךְ הָעוֹלָם, הַמּוֹצִיא לֶחֶם מִן הָאָרֶץ.

Joy watched Ponth and Sarah close their eyes and lower their heads at his prayer. She did the same.

When Jake finished, he stared at the open pizza box that was situated so the lid faced him and Joy. On the lid, in clear red letters, read: ∀IᴚƎZZIԀ ⅄⊥INᴚƎ⊥Ǝ. Jake rotated the box and the smell of crust and mozzarella and tomato sauce brought a tear to his eye. But he retained self-control and gestured to Joy. "Please," he said. Joy kneeled beside him and gingerly pulled out a slice. Sarah's eyes softened. "He's a good boy," she muttered to Ponth. Jake looked up at her and Ponth and pointed at the pizza.

"Nope," Ponth said. "That's all you, big guy. And while you're eating, there's no good a time as any to provide you with the parameters of your first mission."

Sarah did a double take and glared at Ponth. Ponth ignored her.

Joy swallowed a hunk of cheese. "Our first… ?"

"That whole *Freedom Fighting* reference in the title?" Ponth said. "Not just there to sound cool. And we don't have much time to get you prepped."

The muffled sounds of cartoonish gunfire reached everyone's ears from the bedroom. "Thought I turned your TV off before we left," Joy mumbled with crust in her mouth. "Leave it," Jake said. "Landlord pays electric and utilities."

He finished his first slice and peered up at Ponth. "You promised us answers. And that whole thing with the whale that no one else physically sees in an abandoned aquarium kinda, maybe, with no definite uncertainty, just generated a lot more questions."

Ponth nodded. "That's usually what answers do."

"Soooo, we should just give up and say, uh, I don't know, there's no point in seeking answers because it'll just keep generating more unanswered questions?"

"They are not ready for any mission, Ponth," Sarah said under her breath.

"And you know," Jake said. "I love it when people say things under their breath about people like people ain't in the same room. I can hear you, ma'am."

"I know you can hear me."

"It's all good." Jake waved his hand. "I'm not upset. I got food. I'm as happy as a clam in high tide before global warming."

Joy nearly spit out a chunk of pizza. Here was yet another side of him she hadn't seen before. He did have a sense of humor. She made a mental note: Make sure he eats.

"I'm just saying," Jake continued through mouthfuls of what must have been the best pizza he'd ever had in his life, "what's the dealy-deal, man? You're talking about us going on a mission, but how can we even be mission-ready? We're in a state of complete confusion. What are we supposed to do? Blindly trust you and follow orders? I'm sorry. I've seen where that leads. I am not following orders ever again from anyone I don't know. And I don't know you, Ponth J. Sahib. Who are you?"

Joy shifted, not comfortable with the possibility of yet another coming conflict. But she couldn't help agreeing with her new friend. "He's got a point," she said. "Maybe two."

"He does," Ponth conceded, and sat on the couch before the coffee table. "Look, I'll tell you anything you want to know about me."

"Anything?" said Jake.

"Sure."

Jake turned to Joy and they huddled and Jake said under his breath, "Okay, let's talk under our breath like they can't hear us even though we know they can."

Joy giggled. Ponth smiled patiently. Sarah rolled her eyes.

"This is an opportunity," Jake said, "to see how genuine he is."

"Then," Joy replied, "we have to ask him something really sensitive. Something he'd be deeply and overwhelmingly embarrassed to discuss."

"Oh, oh," said Jake. "I got it. Read my mind."

"Already did."

"Let's do it," said Jake. Then he and Joy faced Ponth and said at the same time, "What's your middle name?"

Ponth's face dropped. "Dammit."

The Twin Chickens shouted with glee and shoved more pizza down their throats. "No," said Joy, "not 'Dammit.' Your name isn't Ponth *D*. Sahib."

"Come on," said Jake. "What is it? Jane? Jasmine? Juniper? Jupiter?"

"June?" said Joy. "Jacinto? Julian?"

Ponth shook his head. "Jett."

The Twin Chickens stopped laughing. "Jet?"

"Jett. Two *T*'s."

Jake said under his breath to Joy, "That's actually a cool name."

"It is," said Joy. "Not embarrassing at all."

"Not sure why he doesn't call himself Jett Sahib. That's badass. Way cooler than Ponth."

"But then we'd have a *J* problem," Ponth said. "Joy. Jake. Jett? That can get confusing."

"I'm not confused," Jake mumbled as he finished off another slice.

"No disrespect, big guy, but you just admitted two minutes ago that all you are is confused." Ponth pulled a folded piece of paper from his jacket pocket. "Hopefully getting you two out in the field will help you figure some things out. Little OJT, on-the-job training, you know?" He unfolded the paper and held it up. It was a full-page color ad for a Spiritually

Uplifting Communal and Destiny Intensifying Conference to be held at the downtown waterfront park. "This is happening tomorrow," Ponth said. Then he pointed at the bald, smiling monk in the ad. "You know who this is?"

Sarah looked at Ponth and shot daggers from her eyes. Luckily, those daggers were not discharged at a particularly high velocity and Ponth was able to duck. "Whoa!" the Twin Chickens exclaimed as the two daggers lodged themselves in the wall behind Ponth, who shouted, "Damn it! I know you're displeased, but—"

"I'm sorry!" Sarah said. "I didn't mean to—"

"Weird shit is always gonna happen around these two, so can you please find less violent metaphors to express your anger with me?"

Steam billowed from Sarah's ears.

"Much better," said Ponth.

"Not really," said Jake. "This place tends to get moist 'cause we're in a basement and now you're humidifying it—"

"Mold problems," said Joy.

Jake nodded. "I've had 'em before."

More steam rolled out of Sarah's ears.

"I think that's the best we're getting for now." Ponth held up the picture of the monk again. "Okay, do you know who this is?"

Joy nodded and beamed. "Agh!" Jake yelped, and shut his eyes. The light from Joy's beaming face temporarily blinded him. Sarah shook her head, which began to whistle like a tea kettle as steam continued to pour forth.

"Holy..." Ponth said. "Cool it with the metaphors for just a minute, please!"

Jake rubbed his eyes and blinked. Sarah glared. Joy smiled.

"Of course we know who that is!" Joy said, making an effort to not have stars appear in her eyes. "That's the—"

"The Ladee Dada," Jake broke in.

Joy slapped his shoulder. "Don't call him that. He's the—"

"Ladee Dada. That's what I call him."

"He's not the—"

"Whatever," Ponth broke in. "Then he's the Ladee Dada.

And your mission, Chickens, should you choose to accept it…"

A few seconds passed. Jake leaned toward Joy and said under his breath, "Why won't he finish his…"

"I will," Ponth said.

"When?"

"Isn't it more fun waiting and wondering what I'm going to say this mission is?"

Joy nodded vigorously and grinned. Jake shrugged and took another slice of pizza.

Steam continued to billow from Sarah's ears.

***

"Alrighty," said Hip Gnosis, still standing with his back to Madelyne and the four members of the Executive Board, who sat at the conference table in his office suite. He stood by his floor-to-ceiling window, looking out at the expanse of his corporate campus. "Let's war-game this shit!" he proclaimed.

"I'm recording," said Madelyne.

"Go, Ekron," said Hip Gnosis.

"Exercise. Exercise. Exercise," Ekron said. "This is a tabletop exercise in preparation for the deployment of the Nirvana Protocol in T-minus twenty hours, when the Target will be present at a Spiritually Uplifting Communal and Destiny Intensifying Conference. EAD Milcom will run point on the offensive strike. EAD Belhor will run point on defensive countermeasures. EAD Mammon will run point on post-kinetic follow-through. Milcom, go."

Milcom raised his voice. "The Target was born in the center of sustained symmetric and asymmetric conflict, which my department successfully ensured the proliferation of throughout the overwhelming majority of the domain."

"Kudos on that, by the way," Hip Gnosis quickly whispered.

Milcom nodded. "My department further leveraged this strife on the nation-state level to influence the standing of an operational unit already present in the vicinity of the Spiritually Uplifting Communal and Destiny Intensifying Conference. At T-minus twenty, that unit will be given a mission go, and kinetic action will be initiated from a maritime launch locale."

Hip Gnosis rapidly clapped his hands as if he were a pre-pubescent child sighting their favorite pop star. "Yay!" he said with candescent glee. "Now what about the Target's defensive countermeasures? Personal security detail? Venue hardening? Ingress and egress access control?"

Ekron replied, "Belhor, go."

Belhor sighed. "Yeah. Well, while Milcom was doing his thing, my department did mine. The Miscommunication Unit helped a lot with corrupting the Target's messaging over the years too. So now the sitch is, most of the people in that crowd are going to be in complete chill mode. But that's only the crowd. And the Target, though he likes to say 'violence is obsolete,' will have a multi-layer security cordon. We're talking personal detail, a host-nation-provided protection envelope, then state and local police forces for ingress and egress control."

"Soooo," said Hip Gnosis, "this isn't going to be a cake-walk."

"But it is." Belhor smiled. "While Milcom's been influencing his kinetic strike group, I've been influencing my defensive chill group."

"Defensive chill… ?" Gnosis asked.

"My chill group." Belhor nodded. "It's going to turn the crowd against the security forces."

A sharp laugh exploded from Hip Gnosis. "Damn my eyes, Brother Belhor, for ever doubting thou! Now I—"

"Thee," Madelyne muttered. "Singular objective."

"For ever doubting thee!" Hip Gnosis corrected himself. "Now I see the pattern in the tapestry of…" He trailed off, confused.

"Thine," Madelyne said.

"In the tapestry of thine machinations! And that shit is what's uuuuup!"

Belhor reached his fist across the table and Milcom bumped it with his own. "Me and Milcom have been coordinating a lot since this all started."

"Cross-divisional collaboration," Hip Gnosis squealed. "I'm loving the synergy! Now… let's play out the final stroke."

"Belhor's forces will neutralize security," said Ekron.

"Milcom's forces will neutralize the Target. But none of that will matter unless our follow-through is successful. Mammon, go."

Liz Mammon took a breath and smirked. "While the boys have been playing with themselves, I—"

"Come on," Belhor interjected.

"Is such innuendo necessary?" said Milcom.

Mammon rolled her eyes. "While Belhor and Milcom have been coordinating defense and offense for the kinetic phase of the—"

"Way better," said Belhor.

"Much more professional," Milcom agreed.

"Are you going to let me finish?" Mammon asked.

"I don't understand why you couldn't start like that," Milcom replied.

"Okay, but are you going to let me finish?" Mammon repeated.

"We're not trying to not let you finish," said Belhor.

"Well try a little harder, from a proactive stance, to let me finish," Mammon said with a glint in her eye. "It'd be a first from either of you."

"Oy," said Hip Gnosis.

"Pause the recording," Ekron said to Madelyne, who reached over and pressed a button on the ergonomically designed conference room recorder on the table. Ekron glowered at the three EADs with the ice-veined fury of an amateur writer with designs of greatness who's frustrated with the reality of bashing their head repeatedly into a brick wall in the attempt to elicit from their too often myopic brain a kindly, non-cliché, yet illustrative metaphor for the cold, yawning glare of someone who is simply just not, fucking, around.

Belhor and Milcom kept their eyes on the table. Mammon fought back a smirk and kept her eyes on the ceiling.

"Are we ready to continue?" Ekron said. The three EADs nodded, seemingly subdued. "This is why I'm a lithosexual," Ekron muttered to Hip Gnosis.

"This is why I'm a virgin," Hip Gnosis muttered back.

Ekron nodded to Madelyne, who restarted the recording.

Mammon spoke, "While Belhor and Milcom have been coordinating their finishing strokes..."

Everyone tensed but remained quiet. She hadn't quite said anything unprofessional. Yet.

"... my department's been preparing for the post-co—" She succumbed to a coughing fit that may or may not have been genuine, while Ekron exuded a grand showing of generous self-control. "Sorry," Mammon said, and winked at the other two EADs. "Something in my throat. My department has been preparing for the post-kinetic aspect of this engagement. The phase upon which our success most crucially hinges. We will not get a second chance here. This is why, all this time, the influencers of my department have facilitated an entire industry around the Target. Movies. Bestsellers. Rock-star-level speaking engagements like the one in T-minus twenty. We've gotten the Target placed on a pedestal, the exaltation of which is second to none. And after he is neutralized, upon that pedestal is where he shall remain. It will be his trap, his prison. It will be how he, like all the others, becomes just another agent, willing or not, working to support the mission and vision of HG Incorporated."

Belhor and Milcom exchanged a look. Then they shook their heads and began to clap. Ekron's gaze softened and they, with Madelyne, joined the applause. As for Hip Gnosis, everyone watched the rears of his shoulders tremble (he still refused to face the group). And when he spoke, they could tell he was crying. "Madelyne," he said, "please, turn the, you know..."

"Exercise, exercise, exercise," Madelyne said. "This concludes the preparatory tabletop—"

"Wait," said Ekron. "There's a question I would like, with respect, to get on record."

"Okay." Hip Gnosis sniffed. "But first, I just need to say... and if my blubbery, big-hearted emotions get caught on tape, so be it. I just need to say how proud, how honored I am, by all your efforts. This could be it. The Target is the last of our competitor's serious challenges. This could be what provides us the monopoly we've been so ardently striving to attain."

"Yes, and on that," Ekron said, "what if the Target is not the last? I've been hearing reports."

"Of... ?" said Gnosis.

"Reports that the Twin Chickens have awoken."

Everyone froze.

"What the..." said Belhor.

"Why were we not... ?" said Milcom.

And Mammon simply scoffed haughtily and trained her eyes back on the ceiling.

"Yeah, soooo..." Hip Gnosis said. "About that... Madelyne?"

Madelyne, fully cognizant this question would likely come up, rose to her feet and faced (of sorts, for remember, she had no face) the deputy director and three executive associate directors. "I won't lie," she started. "The Twin Chickens have awoken, and they pose a threat."

Everyone's eyes widened.

"But," Madelyne continued, "there are several mitigative factors we believe will maintain the efficacy of a successfully executed Nirvana Protocol."

Ekron raised their eyebrows. Belhor and Milcom remained stone-faced. Mammon crossed her arms and refused to take her eyes off the ceiling.

"One," Madelyne said, "the Chickens are extremely early."

"Four hundred years early," Ekron broke in. "The last Shift, which we successfully infiltrated, was only two hundred years ago. The Target of the Nirvana Protocol isn't a Shift. He's simply the last of the great harbingers."

"The whole point of the protocol," said Milcom, "was that by co-opting this final harbinger, we'd establish complete domination. So when the Twin Chickens finally arrived, they'd have no room to tactically maneuver. Then they could be destroyed, easily."

"Or just ignored," said Belhor. "If they're here now... that changes everything."

"Not necessarily," said Madelyne. "They woke up too early. We observed their behavior at St. Veronica's Hospital, and they are extremely confused. So confused, we believe it makes them ineffectual."

"Oh," said Belhor. "Why didn't you start with that? If they're in St. Veronica's then everything's cool."

"Well," said Madelyne, "they did escape."

Liz Mammon finally spoke, "They. Escaped. St. Veronica's?"

"Yeah," Hip Gnosis said sheepishly. "With the help of Sarah and Ponth Jett Sahib."

The executives froze again, with the exception of Mammon, who let out a sardonic chuckle.

"Ponth... Jett..." said Ekron. "Is that what he's calling himself now?"

"We've turned this challenge into an opportunity," said Madelyne. "We've had twenty-four-seven surveillance on the Chickens. We've spotted and identified Sarah and Ponth and transport used by WVFF personnel."

"Have you identified the WVFF command and control center?" said Milcom.

"No," said Madelyne. "But we've identified the Twin Chickens' residence and deployed the Miscommunication Unit, which should confuse them further."

"What it comes down to, my brethren, is this," said Hip Gnosis. "The presence of the Twin Chickens increases the risk that the Nirvana Protocol, if executed now, will fail. But check it, yo. If we wait too long, we'll lose the opportunity before us. The opportunity to establish what we've been working for all this time. It's risk versus reward, baby. I think the potential reward is worth it. That's my vote. Each, state yours. We'll move on what the majority decides."

Everyone looked at Liz Mammon. "I'm a hard no," she said. "Too many unknowns. Who are these Chickens? What are their stories?"

"We're collecting that intel as we speak," said Madelyne.

"But," Mammon replied, "you don't have it yet. No. I say we wait, get more data, then reevaluate."

"And we respect your perspective," said Hip Gnosis. "Milcom? What about you?"

"I agree the reward is worth the risk," said Milcom. "I say we strike, on one condition. I personally engage in the field of operation to deal with the Twin Chickens or the WVFF, should they dare rear their heads."

"Noted," said Hip Gnosis. "Belhor?"

Belhor shrugged and muttered, "I agree with Mammon. We should wait."

Hip Gnosis nodded. "Ekron? What say you, cuz?"

Ekron took a breath and carefully weighed their words. "Apparently, the deciding vote is mine. I would hope that we all remember we've come this far only by acting together, in the furtherance of the shared vision cast by Director Gnosis. And that, come what may, our continued advantage over the competition, and our ability to ward off the threats posed by insurgent agents like the WVFF, will remain within the reach of our enjoyment and utility only…" Ekron raised a finger. "Only if, despite the short-term disagreements of our assembly, we maintain our focus on the long-term objectives of our resourceful union."

Belhor and Milcom bowed their heads and murmured their assent. Mammon remained poker-faced.

"My vote is yes," Ekron said. "I also believe the potential reward at this juncture outweighs the commensurate risk."

Hip Gnosis raised his arms as if he were signaling a touchdown.

Ekron faced Mammon. "I hope we all continue to do everything in our power to execute this protocol successfully."

"At the end of the day, I stand by you all, always." Mammon sighed. "I just hope these Twin Chickens don't turn out to be the fiercest warriors since the Golden Horde."

***

"The Twin Chickens are fucking idiots!" Sarah blurted out, her hand trembling with such discernible violence that Nimrod, the hulking bartender, gently removed the mug of IPA from her grip and, with a worn blue-gray hand cloth, wiped the warm beer spilt by his friend from the ash-wood bar top of his uncrowded establishment.

"Sound like some pretty high-functioning individuals to me," Nimrod said.

"You need to meet them in person," Sarah scoffed, and took her beer back.

"Sorry I missed that. They could really see Levi with their own eyes?"

"That's what they said."

Nimrod ran a finger along an epoxied growth pattern in the ash-wood countertop. "You believe them?"

"Given the wacky shit I've directly observed and experienced around them, yes. I do."

"Well. There you go."

"There who goes? And where?"

Nimrod chuckled. "The decision to wake them was made far above our heads."

Sarah leaned back on her stool. "I still can't get over how much you've changed."

Nimrod looked away. "We all know a lot of this shit is my fault."

"Is that why you didn't come meet them?"

"I had some business to take care of here."

"But if you didn't, would you have come?"

Nimrod shrugged. Sarah shifted, forcing him to make eye contact. "Hey," she said. "You're on the side of the angels now. That's all that matters."

"Yeah. Speaking of which. How's Azi doing?"

"Generally uninterested unless some dramatic death and destruction is about to go down." Sarah sipped her beer. "Same old fucking Azrael."

"Damn. Kiss your mother with that mouth?"

"Kiss my husband with it."

"Lucky man."

"Not so much. You hear anything?"

"About what?"

"About where he is."

Nimrod wiped at a spot on the counter. "Nuh uh."

"I'm really pissed."

"At your husband?"

"Always." She wiped the corner of her mouth with her thumb. "But right now, I'm thinking of Ponth."

"Your work-husband."

She laughed. "Fuck that guy. Every day I have to restrain

myself from wrapping my fingers around his throat and not letting go."

Nimrod let out a whistle.

"Look," Sarah said. "Waking the Chickens and all? Decision made above our heads? Check. Got it. I'll keep the faith." She took another swig. "But making them operational? Now? That wasn't a decision made above our heads. That was a decision made by Ponth."

"He does have tactical command."

"That doesn't make him infallible."

"It does make him indisputable."

"I don't need to dispute his orders to refuse putting my faith in them."

Nimrod raised his hands as if he were showing he was unarmed. "Take a breath."

Sarah's voice trembled. "Those two are really special. I can't watch them get hurt."

"I thought they were fucking idiots."

"They're not idiots." Sarah let out a breath. "They're just babies. Broken, lost, confused little babies."

Nimrod smiled. "No matter what happens, you wouldn't be able to protect them forever."

Sarah gritted her teeth. "You'd be surprised what I can do forever."

Nimrod grunted in agreement. He took the end of his hand cloth and rubbed again at the spot on the countertop. The spot refused to surrender its existence, and Nimrod gave up, dropping the cloth on the counter and straightening his stance as his lungs expanded with a sharp inhalation. He inflated his chest to its full, monumental capacity. "Okay," he said, his voice baritone deep with decision. "What exactly did Ponth tell the Chickens to do?"

***

Joy stared at an enveloping expanse of whiteness, which terrified her, triggering a need to seek some semblance of *something* beyond the nebulous, ubiquitous boundary of her peripheral vision; and this manifested in the opening and closing of the gated ion channels in the collection of axons her abducens nerve comprised. Her lateral recti contracted. Her left eye shifted and encountered only more whiteness. But that was okay, for she could now feel her right eye was still closed.

Perhaps its opening would provide further information.

Her levator palpebrae superioris contracted. She breathed easier. On her far right, she could now see a faded transition of sky blue. Her favorite color. A color that made things make sense. It was a baseline, a normalizer, a reminding agent that the world, though not okay, was at least still here. It was also the color of Jake's bedsheets, which meant, she quickly deduced, that she was positioned on her right side facing the white wall of his bedroom. She sensed a shift of mass behind her and an arm, dense, but feathered like hers, landed on top of her. She smiled. Jake had gone to bed on the sofa in the living room. He must have come into the bedroom in the middle of the night. She was happy he had. Or was it right before she fell asleep when he had entered? She couldn't remember.

The transition from wake to dream was a lot like someone's field of vision; there was the clarity of the events before you, the clarity which dimmed in lucidity away from the center of focus in such a gradual fashion it subtly, without warning or attention-seeking proclamation, became a pregnant nothingness comprising matters of which you were still, thanks to your other senses, highly aware. Joy considered this. She and Jake had an overlapping field of vision. A shared worldview. But they were still individuals, whole and distinct in experience and perception. Perspective? Perspection. As the focus of each shifted away from the center, how different then were the dreams encountered in the individual nothingness beyond their respective peripheries? And no matter how different, how amazing was it that as they each shifted back toward the center, they could see and process and interact with the same incredible, confounding, unexplainable phenomena? Is that what they were at the end of the day—is that what any bodies in partnership, whatever their partnership was, were? Just two eyes. Two eyes on a face they were struggling to see in a broken, foggy mirror.

Jake's voice, warm and masculine with the rasp of morning-new, buzzed through the nape of her neck. "Did we dream the same dream?"

Joy felt a tingle pass from neck to belly, and she scooched closer and grabbed the hand of his that had been cast over her and pulled it into her chest. How had he not made a move on her yet? But at this moment, they were spooning—he had slept beside her, then, upon waking, brought his arm around her. Was this his move? She answered and tried to conceal the apprehensive tightness in her throat, "Did we travel through a wrinkle in time in your bathroom?"

"Yes," he said.

"Was there a whale?"

"There was *the* whale."

"Did Ponth ask us to kill the…"

"The Ladee Dada," Jake said. "Yep."

Joy squeezed her eyes shut, then shot them open again to cast off any remnants of sleep. "Did that really happen? Is that really what he asked us to do?"

"We were both there."

"Yes, but I want to make sure we saw and heard the same thing. Maybe we didn't."

"Good point." Jake removed his arm from around her. She wished he hadn't. He sat up in bed. "Let's go over it," he said. "Ponth had some newspaper ad with the Ladee Dada's picture."

Joy nodded. "For the Spiritually Intensifying Conference for Destiny Uplifting."

"I thought it was a Conference for Intensifying Destiny through the Uplifting of—"

"No, it was a Spiritually Uplifting Conference and Communally—"

"It was a gathering," Jake said. "A big one. Do we agree on that?"

Joy sat up and sighed. "Yes. And it's at the waterfront."

Jake peered at his Fitbit. "In three hours."

"And Ponth pointed at the…"

"The Ladee Dada's…"

"Picture and said…"

They both repeated what they'd heard Ponth say, "Destroy this."

The Twin Chickens' shoulders sagged.

"I'm not killing anyone," Joy said.

"I'm not killing anyone either."

"I wouldn't even know how."

"I know how," Jake said. "I'm not doing it."

Joy took a long, nervous breath. "Good then."

"Good what?"

"We're not going."

"To the Spiritual Destiny Uplift?"

Joy nodded. "We won't go. We're not doing any mission. We're not hurting anyone."

"Maybe we should make our own mission," Jake said.

"Will it involve lemon-rosemary scones?"

"What?"

"Lemon-rose—"

"I heard you," he said. "Why would it… ? That's so random."

"I like lemon—"

"Jotted," Jake said. "In my mental notepad. But no, no scones right now. We should go to the waterfront."

"What for?"

Jake answered, "To warn the Ladee Dada."

"What's there to warn him of if we're not doing the mission?"

"Maybe someone else is," Jake replied. "We don't know who these, what do they call themselves? Fuckin' Worldview Freedom Fighters? They're probably a terrorist organization. Probably a terrorist cell within a terrorist organization."

Joy's eyes widened. "But they're so sweet."

"They asked us to kill someone."

"Levi-not-Levi was so kind," Joy said. "And Hailee…"

"Yeah, what's up with that?" Jake asked. "Looked like you knew them."

"Maybe I did."

"Did you?"

"Did you know Azrael?" she shot back.

Jake froze.

"Yep," Joy said. "You froze when you saw Azrael, just like you are now."

"Let's stay focused."

"Oh," she scoffed. "Now let's stay focused."

"I don't know if I knew Azrael, like I could have, maybe? Or I only knew because… I don't know."

"It was the same with me," said Joy. "Levi-not-Levi and Hailee, they were like, people I knew, or didn't, but should."

"We'll figure that out later. Right now we need to warn the Ladee Dada. The WVFF could have contingency plans. They could be sending others to kill him. This could be part of a bigger plot."

"We should go to the police."

Jake burst out in sardonic laughter. "Excuse me, Officer? Hey, I need to report… There's a plot… these guys, the uh, Worldview Freedom Fighters. Yeah, yeah, they want to destroy the Ladee Dada. How do I… ? Because I talk to them… yeah, all the time. Where? Like, wherever, in my apartment… or at their headquarters, yeah… Their headquarters? It's in an abandoned aquarium… I know there's no abandoned aquarium around here, it's, I don't know, somewhere else… It is real, I was just… How'd I… ? Through a wormhole… in my bathroom. Yeah, the wormhole's in my bathroom… What else is in the… ? I don't know, there was a donkey. And a lamb. I'm pretty sure they symbolized the beginning of the universe… Why? 'Cause the donkey said 'let there be light'… No, no, no, the lamb didn't say anything, just the donkey."

Joy rocked herself and fought back tears. "We saw the same things. We might be crazy, but that doesn't mean it isn't real."

Jake gently took her hand. "I'm not arguing that. I'm just saying no authority will believe us. We have to go ourselves. We have to get to the Ladee Dada."

Joy wiped the tears forming at her eyes and brightened. "It will be an adventure."

Jake smiled. "It will be an adventure."

Joy sprung out of bed. "Let's go, then! Let's get to the waterfront."

"First things first," Jake said, and got out of bed and left the bedroom.

"What... ?" Joy asked, but her question was quickly answered by Jake silently walking into the bathroom and shutting the door.

CHAPTER 10

The public park on the waterfront, like most such places, was named after a dead governor who, like most such people, did the best he could with the life he'd been given. This dead governor was also known to have done the best he could with the death he'd been given, having leveraged the news of his terminal prostate cancer to draw attention to the cause of maintaining urban growth boundaries. The perpetuity of public policy, or lack thereof, notwithstanding—what this governor truly maintained was a healthy and stoic resignation to reality, having been known, within the context of discussing his impending demise, to have stated that one was terminal from the moment they'd arrived. He's also given credit for the passage of the country's first bill requiring a refund value on beverage containers, though this latter accomplishment may have been less so attributable to his principles than to his political guile.

Anywhosie… Our heroes, Jake and Joy, walked under a freeway overpass as they approached Dead Governor Waterfront Park, which was a little up ahead and to their left. The concrete ground-level walls of the overpass—in addition to framing several casualties of the lack of built shelters and affordable housing, casualties who hid in tents pitched beside boxes, bicycles, and bags of refundable bottles and cans—cannily echoed the reverberating overtones of the Tibetan throat singing coming from the park.

"That's so beautiful," said Joy.

"Careful," said Jake, pointing to the ground at their feet. They stepped over a hypodermic needle lying on the sidewalk, lonely and dispatched from its companions beside the wall. They came out from beneath the overpass. Joy focused on the throat singing. Jake focused on the white noise of the freeway traffic. Joy asked, "How come you don't like the—"

"Ladee Dada?" said Jake.

"He's not the Ladee Dada, he's the—"

"Okay." Jake stopped walking. "Pick your battles 'cause I'm

not bending on this one. I call him what I call him and that's not going to change. You don't like it, go home. I'll do this myself."

Joy, having stopped as well, folded her arms. "You are becoming more and more of an unlikeable character."

"I'm not here to be liked. I'm here to get shit done."

"If you hate him so much, why are you—"

"I don't—"

"Stop cutting me off!" Joy exclaimed. "It's like every damn sentence I utter around you ends with a dash that—"

"I'm not trying to cut you off!"

"You just—"

"And I don't... I don't hate the player. I just hate the game."

Joy considered bringing her feathered hands to his throat. "What game? He's a spiritual leader."

"Everyone's got a game. Listened to this guy at a gathering like this once. I was what, seventeen? Thought I'd find some answers. He just went on about how violence was obsolete. Everyone clapped and roared." Jake chuckled. "Violence is obsolete. And only two years later..." He trailed off. Joy gave it a moment, then asked, "Two years later?"

"Doesn't matter," Jake said. "He's got his game. He tells people whatever bullshit blanket statements they want to hear so they feel safe in their virtual reality where there's no conflict and no war."

"Then why are you helping him?"

Jake shrugged. "He's still a person."

Joy shook her head. This Jake Chicken Man before her could be infuriatingly complex. "Fine," she said. "You call him whatever you want. But don't expect me to call him that."

"I never expected... I just expect you to not expect me to call him whatever you or anyone else is expected to call him. I'm my own damn person."

"You go be all your own damn person all you want to be! But don't snap at me! And don't, oh shoot..."

Two bat-monkey-cherub creatures had appeared, one on each of their left shoulders.

She felt the wings of the one on hers flutter near her cheek.

She spastically waved her hands about her ears. "No," she said. She spastically waved her hands about her ears. "No," she said. "I'm not going to spastically wave my hands about my ears."

She closed her eyes and took a breath. Jake begrudgingly waited, caring less about the creature on him that chirped with demonic glee.

"We agreed on three things when this started," Joy said, and held up her left index finger. "We stick together. No matter what."

Jake sighed. "You're right. I'm sorry I told you to go home. That was wrong."

Joy held up two fingers. "And you have to be kind to me."

"You have to be kind to me too."

"How am I not—"

"You're not accepting—"

"Stop cutting—"

"Sorry," Jake said. He took a breath. "I'm sorry. What were you going to say?"

"How am I not being kind to you?" Joy asked.

"I need you to accept that I'm not going to see every single thing the same way you do," Jake answered. "Even if we do have a shared worldview."

Joy nodded. "You're right." She held up three fingers. "I just want this to be fun. That's the third rule, remember? We have to try to have fun."

Jake cocked an eyebrow. "Me calling this jackass the Ladee Dada is how I have fun."

Joy threw up her hands. "Fine." The bat-monkey-cherubs disappeared with a *poof*.

"Fine." Jake smirked.

"Okay." Joy laughed and they continued toward Dead Governor Waterfront Park.

"Fine," said Jake.

"Great."

"Fine."

"Okay."

"Fine."

***

Madelyne stood by the conference table at which the four members of the Executive Board still sat. She tapped her phone. "We've got something."

"And what, pray tell," said Hip Gnosis, his back, as always, facing everyone. "Is this something that we've got?"

"Tactical Intelligence Report," Madelyne responded. "Just disseminated. Our SIGINT analysts assessed with a medium-to-high level of confidence that the Twin Chickens just arrived at the SUCADIC."

Hip Gnosis cocked his head to the side. "The suck a what now?"

"The Spiritually Uplifting Communal and Destiny Intensifying—"

"Yeah, that's too... the SUCADIC. Got it."

Liz Mammon scoffed. "And everyone gets mad when I... whatever. You said you had twenty-four-seven surveillance on the Chickens."

"We do," said Madelyne.

"Then how did they get from their residence to the..." She cleared her throat. "The SUCADIC. Unseen?"

Madelyne faltered. "Surveillance isn't perfect. Our team could have missed them leaving."

"Or," said Mammon, "these Twin Chickens, the prophesized—"

"Prophesied," Belhor smugly corrected her.

"Prophesied," Mammon said, and rolled her eyes, "manifestation of a Conscious Shift are highly adept combatants. How did surveillance just not see them?"

To Madelyne's relief, Ekron broke in. "We can hotwash after the operation and drill down on our weak points. Right now, let's deal with what we're dealing with. You said the analysts had a medium-to-high level of confidence. How are they so sure? What telemetry are they using?"

Madelyne looked to Hip Gnosis, who waved his hand as if granting permission.

"Ego flares," Madelyne responded. "And they both just had a large one right outside the SUCADIC."

Ekron blinked, taken aback. They addressed Hip Gnosis, "You can monitor the humans' egos now?"

Hip Gnosis shrugged. "That's how papa do what he do, baby."

Ekron faced Milcom. "SIGINT falls under your War Department," they said. "Did you know about this capability?"

Milcom nodded. "How do you think we've influenced the humans to uptick their disinformation campaigns against each other?"

"I wish I'd been apprised," said Ekron.

"Not Milcom's fault," Hip Gnosis said. "We kept that jizzy-jam uber hush-hush. Milcom reported only to me."

"Only to you?" Ekron asked, and bore their gaze down at Madelyne, who looked away.

Mammon grinned. "I thought right now we were dealing with what we're dealing with."

Ekron narrowed their eyes. "Milcom. Perhaps it's time you graced the SUCADIC with your presence."

"I'm already there," said Milcom.

"Belhor," said Ekron, "unless Mr. Gnosis objects, I think it's best you join Milcom to ensure your group does what it must."

"I concur," Hip Gnosis said.

"Done," said Belhor. "I'm there."

Ekron nodded. Everyone took a breath. An awkward, silent minute went by.

"Updates?" Ekron asked.

"Not yet," said Milcom. Another silent minute went by.

"Hey, sorry," said Madelyne. "I'm a little…" She pointed two fingers at Milcom and Belhor. "I'm not trying to, I just thought, are you guys going to… go? Or…"

Hip Gnosis chuckled. "They're like me. They can be in several places at once."

"Ah," said Madelyne. Then she faced Mammon, who sat beside her. Mammon appraised Madelyne with a mysterious smile. "Are you," asked Madelyne, "also, anywhere else?"

"Oh, honey," Mammon purred. "You have no idea."

If Madelyne had a face it would have blushed.

"Heads up," said Belhor. "We might have contact."

***

"Please have all bags open for inspection," the security guard at the entrance gate to Dead Governor Waterfront Park called out, his blue shirt and cap identifying him as a member of the private patrol company supplementing the police officers roaming the area. "No glass bottles. No alcohol, tobacco. No controlled substances. Only factory-sealed water bottles allowed."

"Fucking fascists," a man in the line behind Jake and Joy mumbled. The feathers on the back of Jake's neck stood up. The throat singing echoed louder. The crowd in the park let out a roar of applause. Joy patted Jake's arm excitedly. "I think he's on stage!" The line moved up.

"Anything on you?" the security guard asked the Twin Chickens, impassively scanning their figures with his metal detecting wand. Joy shook her head. Jake said, "No, sir." The guard waved them through. The throat singing died down.

The Twin Chickens entered the park. Joy was immediately captivated by the stage set up on the south end of the great lawn. She pulled Jake through the crowd toward the stage, upon which the Ladee Dada, stooped and robed in red and yellow, brought his palms together and lowered his brow to another thunderous round of applause. Joy patted Jake's arm again. The monk cleared his throat. Silence blanketed the crowd on the great lawn as the grating crackles of breaking phlegm echoed through the sound system. The Ladee Dada smiled and opened his mouth and said:

"Blah, blah, blah. Blahblah blahblahblah. Blah blahblahblahblah blah blah. Blah!"

The crowd erupted in a roar of approval.

Joy's smile dropped from her face.

"Uh." Jake pointed awkwardly to the grass at her feet.

"Ugh," said Joy as she picked her smile up off the grass. It was thin and flimsy like cellophane. She smooshed it back onto her face. "Did you hear that?" she asked Jake. "All he said was..."

"Not sure what you were expecting him to say," said Jake. His focus was captivated by everything but the stage. The park was populated, densely, with attendees on beach blankets and lawn chairs. It was a sunny spring day. Most were wearing hats and caps and sunglasses. But, as Jake pointed out to Joy with a jut of his chin, if you caught a glimpse of their eyes...

"Oh no," said Joy, finally noticing the spiral patterns in the attendees' irises. "They're all hypnotized."

"Maybe Ponth was right," said Jake. "Maybe we do need to..."

"No," said Joy. "Who says he's the reason they're hypnotized?"

"Blah blahblahblah blah!" said the Ladee Dada.

"Fuck you, fascist!" a voice called out from behind the Chickens. "It's just some grass!"

Jake and Joy turned to face the line at the entrance gate. The security guard sternly told a man, "No controlled substances."

"I have a card for it!" the man screamed, and a crowd gathered at the entrance gate. "Leave him be, what's the big deal?" someone from the crowd called out. Jake and Joy watched a group of officers converge toward the gate.

And that's when they noticed the skateboarder.

The skateboarder, short and scrawny with long, sandy, scruffy hair, would, under normal circumstances, whatever that meant, not be anyone or anything worthy of special notice. Standing a good thirty meters away from the Chickens by the entrance gate, he took a puff from his designer e-vaporizer with one hand and dropped his skateboard to the ground with the other.

"Thought they said no tobacco," Jake muttered to Joy. "Why'd they let that guy in?"

The skateboarder was too far away to have heard Jake, but he cocked his head toward the Chickens as if he had. Then he put a foot on his skateboard and grinned. The Twin Chickens watched him move his lips. Then they heard his words as if he were directly beside them, whispering in their ears: "Because this guy isn't really here."

"Holy…!" Joy yelped, and she and Jake shuddered as if they'd heard someone scratch their fingernails down a chalkboard. "What was that?" said Jake. "That man…" said Joy. "I knew it! The Enchanters. I knew they were real!" She grabbed Jake's arm as the skateboarder continued to grin. "He's here to hurt the…" Joy whispered.

"Ladee Dada," Jake said, and looked toward the monk on stage.

"Blahblahblah!" said the monk to another round of applause.

"We have to stop the Enchanters," Joy said, and tried to pull Jake toward the entrance gate, where the crowd was now shouting at the officers "Fascists! Fascists! Fascists!"

"Stop," Jake said, and tugged back on Joy. "Look." He pointed to all the officers in the park now running west toward the entrance gate. "That's a distraction."

Joy trembled. "Someone's going to attack him. I can feel it."

Jake pointed toward the east end of the park, banked by the river full of fishing boats, deck boats, and small motor yachts docked by the shore. A US Coast Guard vessel and a County River Patrol boat roved the waters, but… "River Patrol is complacent," said Jake. "They're too far from shore. And you think they searched those docked boats? If there's an attack coming, I bet it's coming from the water."

Joy nodded and she and Jake ran south across the great lawn, dodging the hypnotized denizens and their beach blankets and lawn chairs from which, through eyes covered with patterns of dichromatic swirls, they confoundedly observed the commotion at the entrance gate. The Twin Chickens neared the stage. Its platform, where the Ladee Dada continued declaring his blah blah blahs, stood about eight feet off the ground. Three bodyguards—arms folded, jaws set, in dark suits and shades—stood on the ground beneath the platform. One raised a palm as the Chickens approached. "Guys, need you to step back from the stage."

Joy and Jake excitedly addressed the bodyguard, but they said different things in a staggered manner, so what the guard heard was: "*Please,* we *listen,* think *I,* someone's *love* going *this* to *guy* attack, *I* and *do* the *not* attack *want* is *to* coming *see* from *him* the *hurt* shore!"

The guard squinted. "One at a time, folks."

A gentle tenor resonated from the stage. "I heard them just fine."

Jake and Joy looked up to see the Ladee Dada smiling at them from the platform.

"Oh my god," said Joy.

"Definitely not!" The Ladee Dada chuckled. "Now what is this not-attack of want you say is coming?"

"It's not a not-attack," said Jake. "It's an attack-attack."

"From him?" asked the monk.

"From who?" said Jake, confused.

The monk smiled. "From him from whom you see the hurt shore."

"No, no…" Jake stammered, about to try and explain, but Joy grabbed his shoulder and said, "I think he means him."

Joy pointed toward the river, where an exceedingly tall, broad man garbed in military attire stood by the shore. Jake instinctively positioned himself in front of Joy. He tried to make out which branch the man's uniform associated him with. But with its one-sided, gold-colored shoulder cords, red sash, and knee-high black leather boots, the uniform looked more like a high-end Halloween costume than the outfit of any actual officer. Behind this faux general, several black-clad figures leaped out of a docked motor yacht and sprinted toward the stage.

"Shit, shit," Jake said to the bodyguard. "That's them. That's who you need to engage."

"Guys," said the guard. "Please step back from the stage."

"I can help," Jake said, locking eyes with the faux general, who stood about twenty meters away. "I can—" But then Jake felt all the air flee his lungs. "Get off of him!" he heard Joy scream over the background chants of "Fascists! Fascists!" His back scraped against the grass of the lawn, and he realized he couldn't breathe. The faux general, easily twice his size, now straddled him with a knee in his chest.

How could someone move that fast?

Jake struggled under the inhuman weight as the general wound up to deliver a punch. As the general's fist came down toward his skull, Jake knew the blow would be the end of him.

Then there was a rush of wind and Jake could breathe again.

Two pairs of hands grabbed at each of his armpits, and he found himself on his feet, a trembling Joy on his right, a deeply concerned Sarah on his left.

"Are you okay?" Sarah asked. "Are you hurt?"

"I'm fine," Jake muttered, and looked past Sarah. The faux general was the one on the ground now; above him stood another man, just as large, who clenched his fists and screamed, "What now, bitch?"

"Nimrod!" Sarah shouted at the huge man standing over the general. "Save your celebrity grudge match for later." Nimrod kicked the general's ribs, then walked toward Sarah. The general moaned in pain.

Joy looked up at the stage. The Ladee Dada stared back at her, agape. "Asura!" he exclaimed. "Bless you?" Joy responded. The Ladee Dada smiled. "You are blessed as well." "Oh, thank you, thank you," said Joy. "But where are the attackers from the boat?"

Jake swiveled his head. "Damn it. Where'd they go?"

The bodyguard spoke, irritated. "Enough. Get back from the stage. Now."

"Have patience," the Ladee Dada said to the guard, and sat on the stage, his legs dangling off the platform. "They see things you do not. Please come help me."

The other two guards rushed over and helped the monk down from the stage and to the ground. Nimrod joined the group, and the Twin Chickens stared up at him. Nimrod was at least seven feet tall and well over three hundred pounds. "Huge Shaq-man," Joy called up to him, "thank you for helping Jake."

Jake stayed quiet, staring at the large man with suspicion and curiosity.

"We don't know where the attackers from the boat went," Joy continued. She pointed to the Ladee Dada. "We need to get him away from here."

Nimrod looked at Sarah. "Got just the spot."

"Where?" Sarah asked.

"Yeah, where?" Jake finally spoke. "Somewhere you can destroy him yourself?"

Sarah and Nimrod traded a look. "I told you." Sarah sighed. "They're really confused."

Nimrod pulled out his smartphone. "Y'all gonna have to trust me."

"Why would we trust you?" said Jake.

Joy noticed the faux general on the ground a distance away stirring back into consciousness. "We really need to leave," she said.

"We're not leaving with them," said Jake.

"We're on your side, Jake," said Sarah.

"I don't have a side. I just don't want anyone hurt."

"I know what we need!" Joy exclaimed. Everyone looked at her. "A one-liner!" she said.

"A one... ?" said Nimrod.

"That's what always works in the comic books and the action movies, right? A gutsy, profound yet humorous one-liner that instills trust in the intentions of the newly arrived—"

"Come with me if you want to live," Nimrod said, and strode down the lawn toward the area behind the stage.

"No!" Joy pouted and called after him. "It needs to be original!"

"Then come with me if you want to understand what Ponth really asked you to do," Nimrod called back as he stopped at a porta potty.

"Too long for a one-liner," Joy said to Jake. "But it addresses the underlying conflict, no?"

"I guess it does," Jake grumbled.

The Ladee Dada addressed his guards, "Stay here. I need to travel with these people."

"But..." a guard said. The Ladee Dada smiled and held up his palm. The guard bowed.

The faux general sat up.

"Let's move, people," said Sarah.

They joined Nimrod at the porta potty. He tapped his smartphone, then opened the potty's door. "Everyone in."

"Really?" said Jake. "A bathroom wormhole? Again?"

"Can we even fit in there?" asked Joy.

"We'll fit," said Nimrod.

"Can *you* even fit in there?" Joy shot back.

"Whoa, whoa, whoa," Jake said, and grabbed the Ladee Dada by his shoulders. From their left, the black-clad attackers from the boat had dropped from the trees that dotted the lawn and were now rushing toward them. Jake saw the glint bounce off the blades of the knives the ninja-like attackers carried. "Get in there!" Jake shouted, and shoved Joy and the Ladee Dada into the porta potty. Then Nimrod put his huge hand on the back of Jake's neck and gently pushed him through the door. It reminded Jake of how his father used to guide him as they walked the crowded city streets together, with a firm, gentle hand at the back of his neck.

When a man no longer feels his father's hand, Jake thought, he is lost.

Sarah came in last and shut the door just as an attacker reached it. They heard the black-clad assassin scrape the door with their blade and hiss "Death to the God-King-Dictator."

"Death to dese nuts," said Nimrod.

In the pitch-black darkness, everyone caught their breath.

"We have to work on your one-liners," said Joy.

"Okay." Nimrod chuckled.

Jake coughed. "Smells horrible in here."

"You can step outside if you like," Sarah teased.

"Learned my lesson the first time. Thanks for the offer, though."

A silence.

"Since we are here," the Ladee Dada spoke. "I, in fact, do need to use… I wonder if…"

"One or two?" asked Joy

"I'm sorry?" said the monk.

"Water or rocks?"

"Ah. Well. Not water."

"No," said Joy. "God. No. I mean, I love you, but… just, no. No, no."

***

Madelyne and the four lead executives of HG Inc. sat at the conference table in the Director's Suite and watched Hip Gnosis clench a fist against the panel of his floor-to-ceiling window. A black-chinned hummingbird, its throat a startling shade of purple, appeared directly outside the glass, flitting about with its customary wingbeat rate of seventy flaps per second. Hip Gnosis flexed his fist, opening then closing it again. The hummingbird let out a chirp as its body crumpled like an aluminum can, then fell to the ground below with a thud no one heard. If Madelyne had a face, she would have flinched.

"Someone's angry," Liz Mammon purred. "Do we get the flaming head next?"

"Yesterday," Hip Gnosis responded, "that hummingbird… that adorable, delectable, pulchritudinous little creature, used his beak to stab one of his fellows in the throat. They were fighting over a female. Yes. And please, no offense to any of the individuals here who identify as female, I don't say this to shock or cause discomfort…"

"Which means this will definitely shock and cause discomfort," said Mammon.

"… but that motherfucker," Hip Gnosis said, and pointed to the ground outside the window below, "murdered a nigga for pussy."

Madelyne groaned. "You can't use that word."

Hip Gnosis nodded. "You're right. I'm sorry. Pulchritudinous. Poor word choice. Point is—"

"Hold on," said Madelyne. "You can't just gloss over that. You cannot just, no, you can't use words like those." She looked to the four executives for help. "Are you guys… ?"

"I mean"—Mammon smirked—"the P-word is cool. Sometimes. I like it. But only in specific circumstances, within the conditions of, you know, mutual—"

"I should receive consent from a listening party to say pulchritudinous?" Gnosis asked.

"Stop it, Hip." Madelyne seethed. "You cannot say pussy in a workplace environment. And you cannot say, I can't say it. The N-word. Ever."

"But I invented that word," said Hip Gnosis.

Madelyne froze. "You, invented... ?"

"He did," Ekron chimed in, searching Madelyne's non-face. "An eloquent innovation. Did you not know that?"

"I..."

"How long have you been here?"

Madelyne stammered. "Since... the..."

"If it bothers anyone," said Hip Gnosis, "I won't use it. So check it, my ninjas. My point about the hummingbird..."

"Who stabbed another ninja for..." Mammon winked at Madelyne. "Pulchritude."

"... is that even with and through all the beauty in this realm," Hip Gnosis continued, "there are no innocents. None. I was wrong, all those ages ago, when we last convened. I said we had to convince everyone in this realm that all their needs would be met by us. But, see... they actually do need us. It's the burden we bear. And the agents of our competition lie. They lie. They say our path is the road to perdition. But this realm needs us. We keep it in check. We keep the inhabitants from turning it into hell. We do that. Us." He took a breath. Everyone fell silent, even Mammon. "This is why what we do is so important. This is why we cannot fail. So... Milcom, Belhor... Please... WHAT THE SHIT HAPPENED OUT THERE?"

Milcom and Belhor quietly kept their eyes trained on the conference room table.

"That wasn't a hypothetical— "

"My apologies, sir," said Milcom. "An unexpected deterrent arrived. Sarah appeared."

"You," said Hip Gnosis, "the great Milcom, couldn't handle Sarah?"

"She was with..." Milcom said.

"Who? Little Ponth?"

"Nimrod."

"Nimrod." Hip Gnosis shook his head. "So, what happened?"

"He…" Milcom muttered. "Bested me."

"Nimrod bested you." Hip Gnosis sighed. "Alright. Everyone. You know what to do."

Mammon, Ekron, and Belhor grimly stood and surrounded Milcom. Madelyne watched in trepidation.

Then, the three executives threw their arms around the massive shoulders of Milcom. He began to sob.

"It's okay," said Ekron. "You're not any less of a war-god."

"We're here for you, buddy," said Belhor.

"If you want," said Mammon, "I'll give you some… pulchritude."

"Thank you, comrades." Milcom sniffled.

"Wow," Madelyne broke in. "Yeah, sorry to interrupt… that. But, did you encounter the Twin Chickens?"

Milcom nodded. "They, with the help of Sarah and Nimrod, extracted the Target."

"What happened to the state-sponsored assassins you influenced?" Hip Gnosis asked.

"They were evaded. The Target went to the bathroom and…"

"And… ?" said Hip Gnosis.

"Disappeared. Sarah, Nimrod, the Chickens, the Target."

"Disappeared in the bathroom?"

"Correct," said Milcom. "The assassins have vacated the area and aborted their mission."

Hip Gnosis threw his hands up. "So this was a bust."

Mammon chuckled and returned to her seat. "Told you we should have dug up more intel on the Chickens first. If they're disappearing through bathrooms, that is powerful magic."

"I don't know," said Belhor. "Milcom, maybe you got a different impression, but they seemed kind of… weak."

"I engaged the male," said Milcom. "He felt like a newborn infant. I would have ended him had not Nimrod…" Milcom hid his face in his hands. Ekron rubbed his back. "Shh. It's okay."

"Let's stay positive and salvage from this what we can," said Hip Gnosis. "And what we can salvage, is intel. Belhor, stay at the SUCADIC and monitor the aftermath."

"Done," said Belhor.

"Milcom, leave the area," Gnosis commanded. "Take some wellness time for self-care. Go to, I don't know… Rarotonga or something."

"Yes, sir," said Milcom.

"Hey, I'll go with you," said Mammon. "Which, you know… do you want me to…"

"The red one," said Milcom.

"In the meantime," Hip Gnosis continued, "Milcom, Belhor, give us a full dump of everything you noticed about the Chickens."

"Well, for starters—" Belhor said.

"Before we continue," said Ekron, peering at Madelyne, "I would advise that the intel units are, encouraged, to produce a still pending report on the Chickens with the utmost urgency."

"Concur," said Hip Gnosis. "Madelyne?"

"On it," she responded, and left the room.

"You were saying?" Ekron asked Belhor.

"Yeah, for starters," he said, "they don't actually look like chickens."

CHAPTER 11

Jake and Joy squinched their eyes and looked at their red four-toed feet to avoid the overwhelming sunlight bearing down upon their vision. They stood in the square of a concrete slab, and as their eyes adjusted, they realized they were on a tree-lined sidewalk, standing before a low, two-story brick warehouse whose dimensions took up the entire length of the city block, and whose owners had had it fashionably converted into a series of three adjoining stores: the first, an artisanal stationary shop; the second, a neon-lighted deli with occupied café tables and chairs out front—both the café furniture and its occupants successfully straddling the styles of vintage-chic on the one hand and modern-industrial on the other—and the third…

"I smell pizza," said Jake.

Joy shook her head. They had just crossed a stable bridge connecting two disparate points in space and time. They had just walked over Eternity. And all this man could notice was pizza. But maybe in that noticing there was wisdom. We're always thinking of Eternity as an idea that cannot be understood, something immense. But why? What if, instead of all that, you suddenly find yourself in something like a pizza shop; grungy with a visual aesthetic fitting for its location in the gentrified part of town, but not *too* grungy because then it would fail county environmental health inspection standards—it should definitely not have spiders in every corner. No bugs at all, really. That's very unsanitary. That's how pathogenic bacteria are spread. She once tried to explain that to the Monster while they were working at the restaurant, but he just sneered and noted that with her nose in all those novels and news, she knew no more than he, that is, no more than the noose of his known, knowing, know-y, Joy, no way, nowhere, no one, Joy, no… no…

"Joy," Jake said, and she looked up at him and in his eyes there was gentleness and in his eyes there was fear. "Who is this Monster?"

Joy smiled and faltered and trembled and blinked. "You can hear my thoughts now too?"

Jake nodded. "Loud and clear."

Nimrod, observing, muttered to Sarah, "They just wade in and out of each other's streams of consciousness like that?"

Sarah responded, "Among other things."

The Ladee Dada looked around, clapped his hands like a toddler and giggled.

"Who's this Monster?" Jake asked again.

Joy forced a smile. "That's a long story."

Nimrod gently laid a huge hand on each of the Twin Chickens' shoulders. "A story you gonna have to go through later." He guided them toward the pizza shop before them and grabbed the handle of the door. "Hold up," he said. "If our enemy tracks us here, we're done. I'm talking *done* done. So check your egos at the door."

Nimrod looked at Joy. She thought for a moment, then shrugged. "No, I'm good this time," she said. Then Nimrod looked at the Ladee Dada, who looked back with an impish grin. "Yeah." Nimrod chuckled. "You straight." Then he looked at Jake.

Jake avoided eye contact and clenched his jaw. "That guy in the park. The big one. He, I know how to fight… he… I felt like a nothing…"

Nimrod cupped Jake's face with a powerful hand. Jake froze. It was an unexpected gesture. "Bruh," Nimrod said, "before your ego flares up, let me stop you right there. Don't trip on that. Dude in the park wasn't no 'guy.' That was Milcom. Demons like that are way out your weight class right now. But you gonna get there. Alright?"

Jake nodded, not sure of where exactly this 'there' that he was going to get to was, but feeling better already without even the need to stomp any strange bat-monkey-cherub monstrosities into oblivion. "Copy," he said.

Nimrod looked at Sarah. "I'm fine," she said. "You won't be," he said back. Sarah raised her eyebrows. "Whatever goes down in there," Nimrod said. "Promise you gonna stay cool."

"Okay?" Sarah said.

"I'm serious," Nimrod warned.

"Okay," she said again, confused. Nimrod opened the door. They followed him inside.

They passed a glass display on their left showcasing several pizza pies—plain, Margherita, extra cheese. "Those look good," Jake said. He couldn't eat the pepperoni, but it looked good too. A flour-dusted, white-aproned pizzaiolo stood behind the display and checked the oven and nodded at Nimrod, who nodded back and led the group past the chewing, chatting crowd of customers to a door at the rear of the shop, upon which was taped a stained paper with hand scrawl saying: Employees Only—So Stay The Fuck Out. Nimrod pulled open this door and led them down a grimy (but not too grimy) hallway lit by flickering fluorescent bulbs bouncing light off the red ochre-painted walls. They came to yet another door. Nimrod pulled it open and ushered the group through.

```
INT. ETERNITY PIZZERIA - DAY

The group enters another pizza shop, a
mirror image of the first, with a glass
display to their right.


ON GLASS DISPLAY


Extra cheese, Margherita, plain.


ON GROUP

                      JAKE

          Out of pepperoni?

ON GLASS DISPLAY

Behind which stands a bald, brown-skinned
man with the bearing of a soldier and the
```

affability of a country farmer.

MAN

Grab a seat! We've been waiting for you.

The Ladee Dada stands agape. Jake and Joy notice the singular customer in the shop.

ON CUSTOMER

Gray-haired, dining at a booth with his back to the group.

ON GROUP

Sarah tenses. Nimrod gestures to the man behind the counter.

Nimrod

Twin Chickens. This is—

MAN

Call me Sid.

Sid extends his palm from behind the counter and shakes hands with Jake and Joy.

SID

(winks)

My pleasure. Really.

Sarah takes a deep breath, keeps her eyes on the lone gray-haired man dining at the booth. She shoots Nimrod a look. Nimrod avoids it, gestures to the Ladee Dada.

NIMROD

Sid, this is—

SID

Oh, I know who this is!

He steps from behind the counter, arms outstretched.

SID

Bring it in!

The Ladee Dada bursts into tears, sinks to his knees.

SID

Come on, none of that.

He helps the monk to his feet.

SID

You're the guest of honor here,bro.

Ladee hyperventilates. Jake and Joy trade a wide-eyed glance. Sarah glares at the gray-haired man in the booth. Nimrod shuffles, nervous.

SID

Go sit, guys, get comfy. I'll bring out a fresh pie.

He steps back behind the counter.

SID

Yo, Abe!

The gray-haired man perks up.

SID

Stop being rude, huh?

Abe, without turning, waves the group over. Nimrod leads them to the booth, touches Abe’s shoulder, sits beside him. Sarah sits across from Abe. Ladee sits next to Nimrod. The Twin Chickens sit beside Sarah.

Sarah takes a deep breath. Closes her eyes.

ABE

(eating a slice)

What, now you won’t look at me?

SARAH

I can’t have an ego flare.

ABE

Could at least look at me.

SARAH

Last time I was half as pissed at someone as I am at you right now, daggers shot from my eyes.

ABE

Literally? Metaphorically?

SARAH

Both.

ABE

(to Jake and Joy)

That was you two?

Joy

We think so?

ABE

You have to learn to control that.

SARAH

They just got here.

She opens her eyes. Abe flinches.

SARAH

And you're not the one dealing with them, so you don't get to give them guidance.

ABE

Maybe they need my guidance.

SARAH

Because you've got such a great track record with that.

ABE

With what? Guidance?

SARAH

Your guidance sucks.

ABE

And that is what you never understood.

SARAH

Enlighten me then, O chosen one.

Abe drops his slice. Wipes the crumbs from his beard.

ABE

It's not my guidance. I'm just a follower. Everyone wants to be so big. Everyone wants to be a leader.

He peers at Nimrod.

ABE

Right?

Nimrod looks down.

ABE

We're all followers. All of us. Our only real choice lies in what we follow. I made my choice. Long ago. Before you. Before anything. I made my choice.

SARAH

So did I.

Her eyes well up. Nimrod, Ladee, and the Chickens look on uncomfortably.

SARAH

I chose you. I followed you. Everywhere.

ABE

(shrugs)

Then stop.

SARAH

Box checked.

ABE

No. Stop everything. Stop following me. Stop not following me. Just stop.

Sarah wipes away a tear.

SARAH

Do you even love me anymore?

ABE

Love is…

He takes a breath.

ABE

Like a star…

SARAH

Oh, here we go.

ABE

It doesn't revolve around its beloved world. It pulls its beloved to revolve around it, and bathes its beloved in the light and warmth its beloved needs for all its seasons. But there has to be… distance. The right amount. Too great a distance, and the world grows cold and flies off into the abyss. Too close, and the world swelters under the intensity of the lover's gaze.

JOY

(whispers)

Wow. That was better than Rumi.

LADEE DADA

Or Demi Lovato.

JAKE

You listen to Demi—

NIMROD

(mutters)

Not a good time, guys.

SARAH

(to Abe)

You arrogant… So my job, still, is to revolve around you. While you, what, keep me at a healthy distance? That's what this is all about?

ABE

I never said I was the star.

SARAH

What's the star, then?

She points up.

SARAH

Him?

ABE

(shrugs)

Or Her. Or It.

JOY

No, not 'It.' Too creepy. Some writer ruined that name forever.

SARAH

Writers ruin everything.

(to Abe)

Like they ruined our story on

the Mount.

ABE

Still not over that?

SARAH

(to Ladee and the Chickens)

It wasn't some angel's voice he heard that day. It was just mine.

She cups her hands to her mouth.

SARAH

Hey, asshole. You don't need to sacrifice our baby. There's a ram in the fucking thicket right. Over. There.

Jake and Joy visibly shudder.

ABE

The writers never said angel. They said messenger.

SARAH

Yeah, well, I was the fucking messenger. Me. Sarah. Not—

ABE

Yes, you were.

SARAH

I was written out. Like I'm being written out right now.

ABE

I don't think you're being written out.

SARAH

Then why is this the first time I'm seeing this place? Why are you here?

(to Nimrod)

And why was this kept from me?

NIMROD

Just following orders.

ABE

I'm here, in this place, right now, because I need to be.

SARAH

Says who?

(points up)

Him or Her or—

JOY

Please, don't say 'It.' I still have issues with—

JAKE

Shower drains.

JOY

Right?

JAKE

Oh yeah.

JOY

How do you…

JAKE

I remind myself it was the same dude from *Clue* and *Home Alone 2*. We do need a different—

JOY

Appellation. Yes. Let's use 'That.'

SARAH

Says who, Abe? Says *That*?

ABE

Says everything.

(points his thumb behind him)

You see what's going on out there? What they're doing in my name? In Sid's? In the other Stakeholders'?

SARAH

Then get your ass up and come

out there with me. Follow me for once.

ABE

The damage has already been done. To my name. It's become one of the idols I used to destroy. But not yours. Understand? Your name wasn't written out.

He chuckles.

ABE

It was redacted. Protected. So you can do what you're doing now. Being a messenger.

SARAH

For what message, Abe?

Abe smiles and gestures to Jake and Joy.

JAKE

(whispers to Joy)

What message? I'm so—

JOY

Confused. Me too.

Sarah gazes softly at the Twin Chickens.

SARAH

Yeah. Okay.

ABE

Okay?

SARAH

Okay.

Sid comes over, sets down a large platter with a pizza pie.

SID

Okay! Straight out of the oven.

JAKE	LADEE DADA
(lowers head)	(brings hands together)
Baruch ata Adonai Eloheinu…	Tonpa Lame Sangye Rinpoche—

SID

(to Ladee Dada)

Stop, you're making me blush.

Sid pulls up a chair and joins the table.

SID

Just eat, guys.

Everyone reaches for a slice. Sarah slaps Abe's hand away.

SARAH

You're gaining weight.

Abe looks to Sid for help. Sid shrugs.

SID

Why I got divorced, man.

SARAH

(glares at Sid)

Don't get me started on you.

SID
(smiles)

Yes, ma'am.

He turns to the rear of the restaurant.

SID

Mo! What are you up to? Join us, huh?

ABE

Still in the stockroom?

SID

Pretending to be busy.

ABE

Leave him be.

SID

He's got nothing to be embarrassed of.

ABE

After everything those people out there have done in his name?

SID

Nothing worse than what they do in mine or yours. Definitely not worse than what they do in you-know-whose.

JOY

Yes. About that.

She swallows her bite.

JOY

Is, um… Jesus here—

SID

Shh, shh, shh.

Nimrod makes a cutting motion with his finger.

SID

Ixnay on the J-word.

A HOWLING SOB echoes from the rear.

ABE

Too late.

Jake and Joy freeze.

SID

Darn… S’okay. Not your fault. You didn’t know.

JOY

Know what?

SID

We try not to mention that name…

ABE

Gets Mo a little upset.

SID

J-man was, you know, his BFF.

ABE

Used to walk everywhere together, holding hands.

Jake and Joy trade a glance.

JAKE

What happened?

Abe, Nimrod, Sarah, and Sid look at the pizza pie quietly.

SID

Maybe right now we stay focused.

He touches Ladee's shoulder.

SID

We got to figure out what to do with you.

JAKE

Time out. Look, can we at least get an answer to this?

He reaches across the table, grips Abe's forearm.

ABE

Hands off the merchandise, kid.

SARAH

(to Abe)

Be nice.

SID

Answer to what?

JAKE

You're real.

ABE

Yep. Can you let me go now?

Jake does and looks at the group.

JAKE

How are you people even here?

Abe and Sid trade a look.

SID

Fair question.

ABE

Very fair.

SID

You want me… ?

ABE

Be my guest.

Sid smiles.

SID

You guys like time travel stories?

Jake nods. Joy shakes her head.

JOY

No. There always ends up being an unexplained plot hole somewhere.

SID

Right on. That’s why I like the ones where the hero doesn’t physically travel through time, rather their consciousness does.

JAKE

Yeah, yeah, yeah. Like Wolverine in *Days of Future*—

SID

Exactly. Way more accurate that way. No large, organized collection of matter beyond a few elementary particles could maintain its integrity when subjected to the forces pushing and pulling it through time. But consciousness? With a little bit of concentration, consciousness can go like, anywhere.

JAKE

Including your old bodies in the past. Or your new bodies in the future.

JOY

Wouldn't it be your new bodies in the past? Or your old bodies in the future?

SID

(laughs)

You guys are quick.
Either way, your present consciousness can move to your past-body or your future-body.

JOY

(points at him and Abe)

But your bodies… don't exist anymore.

Abe smiles. Sid laughs and claps his hands.

SID

Right! So if my consciousness

travels back in time to when
I'm a child, it will enter
child-body.

ABE

Not a crazy notion. You do it
all the time.

JAKE

You mean memories?

SID

They're not just memories,
bro. They're the wanderings of
your consciousness up and down
the streams of space and time.
And if your consciousness
travels back in time before
your body was born, then it'll
take the form of… ?

The Twin Chickens look at him blankly.

LADEE DADA

(whispers)

An idea.

SID

(smiles)

Hey, head of the class. You've
had a lot more time to think
about this stuff. Let the new
kids catch up.

JAKE | JOY
Whaaaaaaaaaaaa—? ¿De qué demonios estás—?

SID

Think about it. We're all just an idea. Every single one of us. An idea that gets closer to physical manifestation when your mom looks at your dad and says "Yeah, sure… I don't really have anything better going on right now anyway."

Everyone laughs.

SID

And it works the other way too. Move your consciousness into the future, beyond the death of your physical body, and you will find yourself, once more, in the form of an idea.

Jake and Joy nod, comprehending.

SID

The point of this isn't time travel, guys. The point of this is… we… me, Abe, Mo… the other Stakeholders… we're here because we're ideas. And we're stuck here, unable to dissolve back into the ocean of…

(points up)

… That… like most ideas do, because people out there simply will not let us. Which in and of itself, is, hey, not a bad thing. But… Hip Gnosis… he hijacked their thought processes so much, if we step out there, all hell will break loose. So we're trapped here for now… In Eternity.

He peers at the Ladee Dada.

SID

Which brings us back to you, Mr. Valedictorian.

JAKE

Wait, wait, wait…

JOY

Who is this Hip Gnosis person everyone keeps talking about?

Sarah, Nimrod, and Abe shift uncomfortably.

ABE

He's the mirage in the desert.

NIMROD

He's our enemy.

SID

I don’t really like the term *enemy*.

SARAH

The hell would you call him, then?

SID

Our… strategic competitor.

JOY

Competing for what?

SID

Your consciousness. The very idea of you. The very idea of how every “you” out there, the “we,” should exist. But Hip Gnosis has a weakness. He needs you more than you need him. And right now…

He points to the Ladee Dada.

SID

He especially needs you.

LADEE DADA

I am nothing special.

SID

You’re very special. You’re

the harbinger of a Shift. A Shift that has the potential to defeat Hip Gnosis for good.

LADEE DADA

But I am not the Shift itself. So again, I am nothing special.

SID

You are, man. Because you are just so darn good. Better than any of us here. Certainly better than me.

Ladee presses his forehead to the table.

LADEE DADA

Please! No. You are above all teachers.

SID

You're a lifelong monk. Trust me. You're purer than I ever was. And that's the problem. Your whole life, all that energy of yours has been devoted to representing the coming Shift. You could have laid the groundwork for the whole world to be instantly receptive to the Shift when it arrived. Hip Gnosis knew that. So he hijacked the thought processes of everything around you. His agents got you placed on a pedestal with book deals and movie rights. They scrambled your message for the masses who want cookie-cutter explanations and an excuse to lie around and get high all day. They even stoked some nation-state conflict in your name.

LADEE DADA

That has been… difficult.

SID

And you've been handling it like a champ. But Hip Gnosis was successful in turning you into another idol. Just like he did with us. And his finishing blow was going to be having you martyred.

LADEE DADA

That is why we were attacked.

SID

Yes. You would have been assassinated. Turned into a martyr. Enshrining you on that pedestal forever. The idea of you would have had to come here, with us, to be trapped in Eternity.

Everyone takes a breath.

ABE

Eh. It's not so bad here. The food is good.

SID

But what is bad, is that when the planned Shift arrived about four hundred years from now, Hip Gnosis, having trapped most prior Shifts or their harbingers in Eternity, would have made it basically impossible for the Shift to propagate. So That…

ABE
(points up)

That…

SARAH

(points to her heart)

That…

SID

(spreads his arms)

That… decided to switch gears and try something different. That made the Shift arrive early.

He smiles at Jake and Joy.

SID

That woke you up. The Amazing Twin Chicken Freedom Fighters.

A trumpet BLASTS heroically somewhere in the background. Jake and Joy look around, unable to determine its source.

JOY

Us? We're the Shift? But we're…

JAKE

Screwed up.

SID

(laughs)

We're all screwed up.

JOY

So… what are we supposed to do now?

SID

Get out there and, I don't know… shift things.

JAKE

By what? Killing people? That's what Ponth told us our first mission was.

SARAH

That's not exactly what he said.

JAKE

Ponth said…

He pulls the full-page ad with Ladee's photo from his jacket pocket, SLAMS it on the table, and points at it.

JAKE

… destroy this.

SARAH

He did say that.

JAKE

So then what—

Joy touches his arm. They trade a glance. A LIGHT BULB appears over their heads.

ABE

Neat party trick.

JOY

Ponth didn't want us to kill…

JAKE

He wanted us to destroy…

Jake and Joy grab the full-page ad, tear it into shreds, and throw the fluttering pieces into the air.

JAKE	JOY
… this!	… this!

They high-five each other.

JAKE	JOY
Mission accomplished!	Mission accomplished!

Everyone else bursts into LAUGHTER. The Chickens look confused.

JOY

I feel like they're laughing at us.

JAKE

They are.

JOY

Why? We just, we did it. We destroyed it. Why are you guys… ?

SARAH

Because you're so stupidly adorable.

JOY

Is that a euphemism for adorably stupid?

SID

(still laughing)

You didn't accomplish the mission by destroying his picture. You're on the right track, but it's a little deeper than that. Think about everything we've discussed.

Silence.

JOY

Oh. Oh wait… I think I…

JAKE

What?

JOY

We can't let this Hip Gnosis martyr Ladee, or he'll get trapped here.

JAKE

We already stopped those demons from killing him.

JOY

They could try again. Or Ladee could just…

(makes a sad face)

… die.

LADEE DADA

(smiles)

All is temporary.

JAKE

Okay, so, before he dies, we have to make sure… oh…

JOY

You get it now?

JAKE

Yeah…

The Chickens look at each other and smile. Their faces brighten so much it blinds everyone.

ABE

(covers his eyes)

Oy! Little warning next time?

JAKE

I know what we should do.

He leans over, whispers in Joy's ear. She scrunches her face.

JOY

That's stupid.

JAKE

It'll work!

JOY

It's still stupid. How about instead…

She leans over and whispers in his ear.

JAKE

I like my plan better.

JOY

(points to Ladee)

Let's let him decide.

JAKE

Fine.

Jake and Joy slide out of the booth. Jake walks over to Ladee, leans in, and whispers in his ear. Ladee turns red. Then Joy leans in and whispers as well. Ladee turns redder.

LADEE DADA

I, dislike, both of these options.

(sighs)

But either will work. You are the blessed Shift. You decide.

JAKE

Rock, paper, scissors?

JOY

Or… we can do both.

JAKE

We can, can't we.

JOY

Yes.

The Twin Chickens smile.

SARAH

Alright. So… what's the plan?

CHAPTER 12

Hip Gnosis let out a long exhale, fogging up the floor-to-ceiling window of his executive suite. "I screwed the pooch, y'all."

"It was the right play," Ekron responded.

"No. No. This sitch went ratchet AF, and that's on me. I got to own that."

"I did say we should have—" Mammon piped up.

"Even if we had delayed," Ekron cut her off, "the Nirvana Protocol would have been neutralized by the adversary."

"How so?" Mammon pushed back.

Ekron took a breath. "The Twin Chickens awaken four hundred years early, escape Saint Veronica's with the help of Sarah and Ponth Jett Sahib, who haven't been seen in decades, then slip past our surveillance undetected to extricate our target just as we're about to execute a protocol we established eons ago? And they conduct this extrication with the aid of that damn traitor, Nimrod, one of the few entities besides maybe someone like Azrael, who possesses force parity with Milcom. Now how, how in existence, did our competition so effectively deploy such a tight defensive countermeasure?"

"You're saying…" Mammon trailed off, not wanting to finish her thought.

"Yes. That's exactly what I'm saying. The Worldview Freedom Fighters *already knew* about the Nirvana Protocol."

Everyone froze.

"So," said Hip Gnosis, "there's a mole in our midst."

"That would be the most plausible explanation," said Ekron.

Hip Gnosis's head burst into flames. The four executives pressed their palms and foreheads to the conference table as the room's temperature drastically rose.

"What is beneficial, sir," said Ekron, "is now we know that they knew."

"BUT DO WE KNOW," said Hip Gnosis, "IF THEY DO OR DO NOT KNOW THAT WE KNOW THAT THEY KNEW?"

"Counterintel is so fucking annoying," whispered Mammon.

"Shh," said Belhor and Milcom.

"We do not," said Ekron. "But at least we know we have a mole. We know what the Twin Chickens look like. We know entities like Nimrod are operational again. We have intelligence we would not otherwise have, had we waited and not taken the risk."

"UNTIL WE DETERMINE WHETHER THERE TRULY IS A TRAITOR AMONGST OUR RANKS, EVERYONE MAINTAINS A PRESENCE IN THIS OFFICE AT ALL TIMES."

"Yes, sir," the executives murmured.

"WRITE DOWN ALL OTHER LOCATIONS WHERE YOU ARE PRESENT. IF YOU ARE ALONE IN A LOCATION, BUDDY UP WITH SOMEONE ELSE IN THIS ROOM. NO ONE REMAINS ALONE ANYWHERE FOR NOW."

Mammon purred at Milcom, "I'm alone in one of the tiers of the Pamukkale springs."

"I'm already with you in the Maldives," Milcom responded.

"Can't handle me twice?"

Milcom clenched his fist. "Simultaneously?"

"Ugh," she grunted. "Belhor? Pamukkale? Come keep an eye on me?"

"Fine, whatever," said Belhor. "Milcom, I need you to join me back at the SUCADIC. Like, now."

"What is it?" Milcom asked.

"The porta potty. I've been watching it this whole time. No one else has gone in. Now it's shaking hardcore. I think the WVFF came back."

"They escaped with the Target," Milcom said. "Why would they—?"

"MILCOM," thundered Hip Gnosis. "DEPLOY."

"Yes, sir," Milcom stuttered. "I just… if Nimrod is there again, I…"

"OKAY, OKAY." Hip Gnosis sighed and the flames from his head died down. "Come on, everyone. Who's the baddest one-man cordon this side of the River Jordan?"

Ekron, Belhor, and Mammon shouted, "Milcom!"

"Who's the god of Carthage? Of Ammon? Of Tyre? Of Hinnom?"

"Milcom!"

"Now you tell me, brother Milcom," Hip Gnosis continued. "You look deep in your deep, dark soul and look dark in that dark, deep hole, and you tell me… Are you about the Canaan? Or are you about the Canaan't?"

Milcom stood and roared with the fire and fury of all the world's never-ending wars. "CANAAN!!!!"

"Now you gonna represent?"

"YES!!"

"You gonna fight?"

"YEEEES!!"

"This is round two. Nimrod's coming for you. So what are you, gonna fuckin' do?"

"I WILL EAT HIS FUCKING CHILDREN!"

"Whoooooahh," everyone replied.

"That's a little much, honey," said Mammon.

"We don't do that anymore," said Ekron.

"Yeah, that one was bad for branding," said Hip Gnosis. "Bit of an obsolete marketing strategy there, not one we really want to bring back. I was looking for more of a 'yeahhh, I'm a beat his ass.' We could even do a 'arrrr, I'm a fuck his girlfriend.'"

"No," Mammon said firmly. "It is the choice of the lover of the vanquished whether she, or he, shall lay with the victor. That is no longer the victor's choice. We don't do that anymore either."

"Really?" said Hip Gnosis.

"She's right," said Ekron.

"Sorry about that. Let's just keep it to a safe, inclusive, 'I'm a fuck that dude up.'"

Milcom slammed his fists on the table. "I'm a fuck that dude up!"

"Yeah!" said Hip Gnosis. "Fuck that dude up!"

"Yeah!" Ekron and Mammon echoed. "Go fuck that—"

"Porta potty's opening," said Belhor. "You need to get here now."

***

Sarah, Nimrod, the Twin Chickens, and the Ladee Dada felt themselves in a pitch-black, constricted space—as if they were in a New York City subway car suffering a power failure in the middle of a tunnel during evening rush hour, in summer. And not unlike said discomfiting mode of mass transportation, it smelled. Bad.

"Are we back in the porta potty?" asked Joy.

"Technically," Nimrod answered, "we never left."

"Ew, so that *was* a toilet I just touched."

"Who's near the door?" Sarah said. "Open it already."

"Can't see shit in here," said Nimrod as he scraped his huge hands against the plastic ceiling and walls. "People, feel for the door latch."

They shifted their bodies in the dark and Nimrod lost his balance and crashed into a wall. They felt themselves tip. "Stop. Stop moving," said Jake. "We're gonna knock this whole thing over."

"I have an idea," said the Ladee Dada.

"Yes?" said everyone else as the porta potty righted itself again.

"It seems when our exalted Twin Chicken friends come up with a good idea or attain some form of profound insight..."

"A light bulb appears," said Sarah. "Great idea. Guys?"

"We can't just do it on call," Jake said.

"And we need, um, yeah, a good idea or some profound insight," said Joy.

"What about the idea to come up with a good idea?" asked Nimrod. "That was a good idea."

"But it wasn't our idea," Joy answered.

"Just keep feeling for the door," Sarah said. And everyone did.

"Your Holiness?" said Joy. "I have a question."

"Ask me anything," said the monk.

"When me and Jake got here and you spoke to the crowd... all we heard was blah, blah, blah."

"And?" said the Ladee Dada.

"That's literally what we heard," said Jake. "Blah, blah,

blah. Maybe it was more like blahblahblah blah blah."

"And?" the monk said again.

"What were you actually saying?" Joy asked.

The monk chuckled.

"Soooooo..." Joy and Jake said at the same time, and a light bulb appeared over their heads. Joy giggled. "We were hearing you just fine, huh?"

The monk smiled.

"Good job, Chickens," said Sarah. And now that everyone could see, she flipped the door latch open. "Damn thing was in front of me the whole time."

They all spilled out of the porta potty and onto the grass of the Dead Governor Waterfront Park's great lawn. In the area behind the stage, they gathered their bearings. Jake turned to the Ladee Dada. "You ready?" he asked.

"I suppose," the monk responded.

"Shit," said Sarah. Everyone looked to where she pointed.

Milcom and Belhor approached from the east.

Jake clenched his fists and stepped forward.

Nimrod clasped his shoulder and pulled him back. "You stick to your plan."

***

At the conference table in Hip Gnosis's suite, Mammon asked, "Is it them? Did they return?"

"Yep," said Belhor. "They even brought the monk back."

Milcom shook his head. "I still don't understand why they—"

"Don't look up a gift horse's ass," said Hip Gnosis. "Just ride it 'til it dies."

"We have a second chance," said Ekron. "Mend the mission, Milcom. And make the monk a martyred man."

"And while you're at it," Mammon muttered with a roll of her eyes, "maybe, meticulously, make me a milkshake or a mixtape."

"What was that?" Ekron demanded.

"Nothing," answered Mammon. "I'm going to the SUCADIC too. I want to watch this."

"Our limitations in this domain still apply," said Milcom. "We can engage the entities of the WVFF…"

"But you can't harm the Target directly." Ekron sighed. "What about the nation-state actors you influenced?"

"They left the area," said Milcom.

"How far are they?" asked Hip Gnosis.

"Two miles."

"Well… ?" Hip Gnosis asked.

"On it," said Milcom.

***

The black-clad assassins, quantity of four, rode their wide-beamed, blue-striped, Fountain 32 Thunder Cat powerboat at a mere fraction of its twin four-hundred-horsepower engines' maximum speed, so as not to attract the unwanted attention of the County River Patrol roving the waters while they, the unsuccessful assassins, anxiously placed distance between themselves and the vicinity of their unanticipated failure.

They were heading north-northwest, in the direction of the conflux where they could switch back on the main stem river toward the international airport and quickly clear out of the confines of the continental United States. But then, one of their smartphones smartly sounded. Of course, no one could hear it over the din of the boat's eight hundred horses holding themselves to a halcyon trot; but Milcom, unseen by the assassins—for though they had reached the heights of government-trained badassitude, they were mortal still—arms folded, twin tower-like legs straddling the deck and maintaining his significant bulk in perfect balance despite the unpredictable jerking by the river's eddies and waves, in a voice unheard by the mortals' ears yet still translated by the interpreter of their collective unconscious, said, "Hey! Check your fucking phone!"

Speedboat Assassin Two—who sat next to the driver, Speedboat Assassin One—looked at their phone and saw a tweet notification from the Ladee Dada: *Many apologies for my sudden absence. I will now return to the stage with an urgent and important message for all!* The tweet was one minute and fourteen seconds old and already had 2,129 likes, 783 retweets, and 314 responses. Speedboat Assassin Two showed their phone to Speedboat Assassins Three and Four who sat in the rear. Speedboat Assassin One took a peek as well, then turned the boat around.

***

Joy gave the monk his smartphone back. "I tweeted for you."

"Thank you." He smiled.

"Get him to the stage," Nimrod said to the Chickens as he and Sarah stared down Milcom and Belhor. "We got your six."

Jake and Joy each held a crook of the monk's arms and hustled him toward the platform. Nimrod and Sarah faced the two demons. "I'll take Belhor. You focus on Milcom," Sarah said, and held out a fist. Nimrod bumped it with his own.

"Fighting out of the red cornerrrrrr!" a female voice boomed. Nimrod and Sarah looked to its source and groaned. "Why's this bitch here?" Sarah asked as Mammon sauntered toward them, dressed to the nines, tens, and elevens (but not the twelves) in a black-mesh ruched bardot bodycon minidress and kitten-heel pumps. "Well, she ain't here to fight," said Nimrod.

"Then why's she here?" said Sarah.

"Cheer on her boyfriend?"

Sarah smirked. "Which one?"

Nimrod looked down and muttered, "That was a long time ago."

"Our tag team," boomed Mammon, "consists of a superheavyweight from the land of Shinar and a middleweight from Ur."

"Hey!" Sarah screamed. "I am a fucking welterweight at most!"

Mammon laughed. "King Nimrod! And Sarah the mother of—"

"Fuck this," Sarah shouted as she bolted toward Belhor.

She was even faster than Nimrod. Meanwhile, Milcom flexed his trapezii and let out a growl as Nimrod rushed to meet him on the field.

As for Jake and Joy, they had succeeded in getting the Ladee Dada back to the stage. They stood on the east side of the platform, out of view of the audience, on the great lawn, waiting for Ladee to speak. They stood with the same bodyguard they had interacted with on pages 137-139, who now peered through his dark shades at the two with distrust and concern. "Hey," Joy said, sensing his dubiety. "Can you see our chicken suits?" The guard cocked an eyebrow. Joy grinned. Even in the womb, her mamá had always told her, she had been mischievous. She just couldn't help it.

At center stage, the Ladee Dada waved to the applauding crowd, then turned to his right to see Jake and Joy still on the east side of the platform. He gave them a look as if to say "you sure about this?"

Joy grinned and Jake nodded with vigor, and both raised their pairs of feathered hands in a quadruple thumbs-up.

The monk sighed and looked out at the crowd, into the eyes of the gathering's attendees. There were black-and-white swirls and red-and-green swirls and swirls of fuchsia and teal, but they were all hypnotized swirls in the irises of the sentient beings he had sworn to serve. *Sentient* was a funny English word, the monk thought. In his own language he, clearly, would not call any of these people a sentient being, he would call them *sem chen*, which, if translated properly, meant "being with a mind that is conflicted and confused by thoughts derived from the illusory yet prevalent concept of duality." But that would take too long to say. "Sentient being" was the best possible translation, but aggravatingly enough, *sentient* itself fell into the trap of the aforementioned duality; with its Latin root *sentire*, "to feel," distinguishing sentience from thinking and reason. Hip Gnosis sure did a number on these people when he convinced them their thoughts and feelings were two different things. But at least the root of sentient and sentience remained firm in the ground to nourish the leaves of additional words like *sense*, *sensation, sentiment,* and most curiously, *sentence.* Perhaps *sem chen* should have been translated instead to "sensational being," or "sentimental being," or "sentence-making"... oh... sentence-making being. Now *that* would have been...

"Hey!" Joy whispered sharply from stage left. The Ladee Dada jerked his head toward her, then winced as he felt a pain in his right big toe and looked down. At his feet were the small pieces of a cracked toy locomotive with its cargo car atop a shattered plastic miniature rail. "What is— " he started to mumble, but then he giggled and looked back toward Joy.

"You broke my train of thought," he said.

"Whatever. Stop procrastinating!"

The monk rubbed his belly. "Okay. Don't rush me."

"Yeah, you need to rush," Jake chimed in. "We got incoming."

The Twin Chickens watched a wide-beamed, blue-striped, Fountain 32 Thunder Cat powerboat dock on shore a short distance east of the stage. The four black-clad assassins slinked from the craft. "Damn it," Jake said to Joy. "Make Ladee do it *now*. I'll deal with the assassins."

"And how am I supposed..." Joy started, but Jake had already jumped off the stage.

Meanwhile, back in the area on the park lawn, behind the setup of the stage, the cosmic tag-team battle of titans versus demons continued.

"Belhor's got Sarah in a rear naked chokehold," Mammon shouted at the combatants. "But wait, Sarah's grabbed his foot and she's twisting his ankle like it's the truth! Belhor's grip is loosening. Reversal, she's got a reversal! Sarah's free, now she's working side control. As for Milcom and Nimrod, the two big men remain in stand-up. Looks like they both want to avoid going to the ground. Maybe Milcom doesn't want grass stains on his freshly pressed uniform, but Nimrod, in his jeans and hoodie, came to fight! Nimrod throws a left-right combo, but Milcom slips, returns a jab. Fails to connect! A looping right from Nimrod, misses. Oh! Milcom connects with a low kick. Nimrod stumbles, that woke him up..."

Back on the other side of the stage, Jake realized a few things the adrenaline-filled instant he jumped off the platform to the ground below, a few things that locked into place with proof-like certitude:

Statements	Reasons
1.) It takes a minimal level of athleticism to land from an eight-foot drop safely.	1.) The Parkour Theorem
2.) Jake possessed this level of athleticism when he was eighteen years old.	2.) The Glory Days Theorem
3.) Jake was no longer eighteen years old.	3.) Given
4.) Conclusion: This was a stupid idea.	4.) The Reality of Aging Postulate

"Fuck!" Jake shouted as he landed (poorly) and his legs buckled and he, for some reason, thought about ninth-grade Geometry class with that asshole teacher, what's his name, Mr. Fuckface, who always complained Jake's proofs weren't "elegant," even though they were always right. Stupid, lazy, fuckface teacher who never bothered to get out of his chair from behind his old, crumpled desk in that goddamn bullshit academy named after some goddamn bullshit saint and—

"You okay?" Joy said, peering down from the stage.

Jake stood and hobbled. "Sprained my ankle."

"Walk it off," Joy said, then turned her attention back to center stage and whisper-shouted, "Let's go, Ladee!"

"Walk it off," Jake muttered, and limped toward the black-clad assassins. He closed the distance between himself and his opponents, who, bemused, watched his approach. He was outnumbered. Four to one. And these weren't tired, overworked hospital orderlies. These were clearly the recipients of a high level of government-sponsored training. They had definitely passed through at least the 35th Chamber of the Shaolin Temple, though likely not the 36th or they would have already shoved Jake to the ground telekinetically. And that's where Jake's only opening resided—he could get close to them. And he did. Walked right up to them while Speedboat Assassin One crossed his arms and smiled. Jake smiled back and cracked his knuckles and did the only thing a grown man in a chicken suit facing four dangerous fighters could do.

Meanwhile, back on stage, Joy said to Ladee's bodyguard, "Maybe you should help Jake."

"Help him what?" asked the guard.

"Fight the assassins."

"Looks like he's doing fine to me."

Joy turned to see Jake on the lawn and her mouth dropped. (She managed to catch it mid-air this time, before it hit the ground, and put it back on her face.) He was dancing. He was dancing hardcore. The Running Man. The Sprinkler. The Vogue. A horribly uncoordinated attempt at the Floss. And now he was doing the Macarena.

"Oy," said the bodyguard. "Little bit of a throwback there."

"Dios," said Joy. "He's terrible. Listen, he's only distracting them. Please help him!"

"Distracting who?" said the guard.

"I told you, the assassins!"

"All I see are four tourists laughing their asses off at your friend."

Joy gave up on the bodyguard and whisper-shouted to the Ladee Dada, "Your Holiness, please. Jake has no rhythm and not much of an imagination. He can only hold them off for so long!"

The monk sighed and nodded and faced the crowd. He gazed with great sadness once more at the hypnotized swirls in their eyes. Hip Gnosis had used him. Co-opted him. Twisted his image, his life, his words, his deeds, into yet another cause for division when he should have been an arbiter for awareness, for acceptance of reality. These strange Twin Chickens, who somehow saw things as they were, with no filter between perspection and phenomena, were right. Drastic measures were necessary. And the time to act was now.

"Let's rock and roll," the monk said to himself. Then he smiled at the crowd and said, "Blah, blah, blah." Everyone cheered. He turned to the side so all could view him in profile, leaned forward, bent his knees, and hiked his robes above his waist.

On the great lawn, an assassin looked past Jake's flailing, feathered dance, pointed to the stage, and let out a shout of dismay.

On stage, Joy covered her eyes with a plumy hand.

The crowd gasped.

And Ladee smiled. His internal and external anal sphincters relaxed as colonic peristalsis initiated. His eyes rolled upward. His vagus nerve, pudendal nerve, and prostatic plexus fired signals in waves. The crowd murmured in confusion. Some laughed, nervous. Then there were cries of disgust as the monk's excrement—long, thin, and contiguous, with a slightly yellowish tint from the light breakfast of tsampa and po cha he'd eaten that morning—exuded from his anus and spooled onto the stage. There came jeers from the crowd. But the monk simply blinked and twitched his face in pleasure as he completed what he had begun. Then he stood, dropped his robes, ignored the boos, and gazed upon his handiwork. It was a perfect shit. It was a divine shit.

It was a holy shit.

And it worked. His bodyguards appeared and whisked him backstage, but not before he looked at the crowd one last time and saw that not all, but many, blinking profusely and looking about in astonished bewilderment, had lost the swirl pattern in their eyes. Not all. But many. And many was a damn good start.

The black-clad assassins shook their heads in defeat and turned their backs on Jake, who had indeed exhausted all known dance moves and was now repeating the Running Man. Dejected, the assassins maundered and meandered back to their boat, then drove away. Jake looked to Joy on the stage. They caught each other's eye and laughed and pumped their arms in the air and shouted with all their might and glee:

"Mission accomplished!!!!"

On the lawn, in the area behind the stage's setup, Mammon's mouth continued to run. "Belhor needs to get out from under her! Sarah's grounding and pounding his face like it's commercial-grade beef. As for the other two, Nimrod just connected with a right. Milcom stumbles! Nimrod presses forward, banging to the body, and… shit! Something's wrong!"

"Yeah," Belhor shouted, trying to block Sarah's barrage of blows. "The monk, he… let's just go. It's over. For now."

Milcom roared at Nimrod, "I'll have your head yet, traitor!" Then he and Belhor vanished, not with a lap dissolve effect, but with more of a jump cut. One instant they were there. The next, they were gone.

"I think you undisputedly beat his ass, big man," Mammon said, strolling toward Nimrod in her dress and heels. "Want to fuck his girlfriend?"

"Sarah," Nimrod called out, his hands on his knees as he caught his breath. "If I punch her in the face, I'm going to become a highly unlikeable character."

"I got you," Sarah responded as she jumped to her feet and rushed toward Mammon. But the wanton demon vanished before she could be reached.

Joy came sprinting up the field toward Nimrod and Sarah, a hobbling Jake in tow doing his best to keep up. "We did it! We did it!" Joy sang-screamed, then skipped like a schoolgirl to her own exclamatory decree. Sarah grabbed her into a hug and kissed the top of her head. "We know, sweety, you did great." Nimrod pointed at Jake's feet. "You okay?" Jake nodded. "Just a sprain." Nimrod clapped Jake's back. "Good work." Jake stumbled forward from the force of the big man's hand and tried to ignore not so much how small he felt, but how oddly comforting that feeling of smallness was. Joy, meanwhile, prattled tirelessly, "Ladee was being like, procrastinatory, and I was like 'Do it! Do it now!' and Jake was like 'The assassins are coming!'"

Jake suddenly jumped in, "Then those fools were all 'Yo, my kung fu be better than your kung fu' and I was like

'Whaaaaat, sucka!'"

The Twin Chickens laughed, their words running into each other again. "Your *and* kung fu *that* ain't *stupid* better *guard* than *goes* my *I* kung fu *see* if *nothing* we *and* do *I'm* the *like* dance-fu *now* fool *Jake* so *is* I *dancing* busted *do* my *it* moves *now*!" Jake started doing the Sprinkler again, Joy, a much better version of the Floss. Sarah and Nimrod shook their heads. The Chickens said simultaneously, "And Ladee did it! And all those people got dis-illusioned!"

Sarah smiled. "Careful. They weren't fully disillusioned. Just a bit startled awake."

"Most of them gonna relapse," said Nimrod. "They'll attach to something else."

Jake and Joy deflated. "Then what do we do?" asked Joy.

"Stay on the offensive," Sarah answered. "We've got the enemy on their heels. We push forward. We keep fighting."

Jake and Joy exchanged a look and smiled. "We can do that," said Jake.

"Good," said Nimrod, and he pulled out his smartphone. "Now, let's make like a modern economy and disappear."

"Better one-liner," said Joy. "Original, but a little forced. Kind of over-intellectual."

Jake shrugged in apologetic agreement. Sarah laughed. Nimrod tapped his smartphone and let out a chuckle. "I'll keep working on it."

CHAPTER 12

Yes, we know the last one was Chapter 12 but 13 is such an unlucky number and 12 is such a holy number and…

Anyways… There was a door. (Yes, yes, we know, we promised… no more "there was a [insert noun]" introductions. But are not promises, dear friends, little more than desperate notions put forth for the purpose of pretending control?) So… There was a door.

The door was one and three-quarters of an inch thick, eighteen-gauge steel assisting the attainment of a sound transmission class above fifty for the room it concealed. Below the sign affixed to the door, reading *"Intelligence Unit – Authorized Access Only,"* was a high-security deadbolt combination lock which, if spun properly, would gain one entry to a windowless office dotted with islands of forty-two-inch-tall cubicles—low enough for the allowance of employees inhabiting the grown-up cubbies to stand and face each other in productive interaction. (Synergy!)

In one of these cubicles, one of these employees organized a stack of papers, then dashed to an alcove at the other end of the floor where Madelyne, the special assistant to the director himself, stood at the desk of a printing station and pressed a pamphlet with a spiral hole punch. "Finished?" Madelyne asked, and the employee held out his stack with a trembling hand. For he'd just realized that not only had he kept Madelyne waiting, but Deputy Director Sam Ekron themself—arms folded and leaning against the printing station—waited impatiently as well. Madelyne took the stack of papers. "Thanks so much," she said. The employee smiled uncomfortably and turned to go.

"Wait," Ekron said, and the employee froze. "How long have you been with us now?"

"Not long," the employee turned and answered. "But to be honest, time gets a little murky here."

"And what did you do before?"

"Before?"

"Before you joined HG."

"Pretty similar work to this. I think."

"Not surprising."

"Surprising to me," said the employee.

"How so?"

The employee looked down. "I'm not complaining or anything."

"I enjoy rank-and-file honesty."

"Well, in my last job? I was just following orders. I remember that much. So when I was told I was getting sent, you know, here, I was a little taken aback."

"Was it our company's reputation?"

"It is a little intimidating."

"We need to do a better job with that."

"I think so. 'Cause, honestly, it's been great here. Not what I expected. At all. The work-life balance, flex schedules, telecommuting options..."

"Do you feel supported in your career development plans?"

"Absolutely. And the morale is great. The free gym helps. And the café's pastries are to die for. I have to not give in to eating a lemon-rosemary scone every meal. And there's... oh, wow..."

The employee trailed off. For without warning had appeared a long-haired man in a white robe. And though this man stood facing a wall of the alcove so that his back was to everyone, the employee immediately recognized him.

"Director Gnosis..." the employee said.

"Call me Hip," Gnosis responded. "I don't mean to be rude or imposing, but could you continue this conversation with Sam at your workspace perhaps?"

Sam Ekron shot a look at Madelyne, then faced the employee. "Come," they said, and led the employee from the alcove. "You can show me what you're currently working on."

"You look really silly facing the wall like that," Madelyne said.

"Yeah," Hip Gnosis responded. "Should maybe get some windows up in this joint."

"You know we can't do that."

"Everything in this unit is so darn sensitive."

"You could just face me," she said.

"Not yet."

"I miss your face."

"I miss yours too."

"Then give it back," she said.

Hip Gnosis took a breath. "Not yet."

Madelyne punched holes in the papers the employee had handed to her. She collated them amongst six stacks on the desk. "Ekron doesn't trust me."

"We might have a mole."

Madelyne nodded. "Ekron told me."

"I made everyone buddy up until we figure this out."

"And Ekron jumped at the chance to keep an eye on me."

"Would you have rathered one of the others?"

"*Rathered* isn't a word."

"Would you have preferred—"

"I would have rathered you."

Hip Gnosis sighed. "Not a good optic."

"Do you trust me?"

"Can I?"

Madelyne thumbed through one of the stacks. "Have I ever given you reason not to?"

"Things have changed."

"Not for me."

"You positive?"

"As a heroin addict's HIV test."

"That was..." Hip Gnosis burst into laughter. "Aw shit. That was good."

"Little too dark maybe."

"Keep the dark. I love the dark."

"I love you," she said.

Hip Gnosis paused. "I love you too, shawty. I just need to make sure."

"Of what?"

"That you feel okay. Now that the Twin Chickens awoke. I asked you before. How do you *feel*?"

Madelyne spiral bound one of the six paper stacks. "Don't know why their appearance would make me feel any different. It's me. I'm not one of the weak-minded idiots of this domain."

"I know that."

Madelyne held the booklet out. "You get the first copy. Intel hustled and pulled a lot together."

Hip Gnosis took the booklet without turning around. "This is everything on the Chickens?"

"Everything so far. Some photos. Open source. Driver's license for the female. Old online dating profiles."

"Let's get this to the others," Hip Gnosis said.

"Sure. Let me put the rest of—"

"Nah, let's just make like a line break and jump to the next scene."

"What do you—"

***

Madelyne stood at the conference table in the executive suite of HG Inc. with a banana, five spiral-bound pamphlets, and a tall caramel macchiato with a dollop of preternatural anxiety. She avoided the gaze of Deputy Director Sam Ekron, trying her best to not appear as if she were avoiding it, and noted, knowing what was coming next as she took her seat, that at least Director Gnosis's head was not aflame.

"Soooo," Gnosis started, still facing the window. "Is it only now that everything's shot to shit or were we kind of already there?"

"I was winning this time," Milcom said. Liz Mammon chuckled. "I was," Milcom whined.

"Doesn't matter who was winning," said Belhor. "Nimrod and Sarah drew us into a fight to keep us from the Twin Chickens."

"Then," Hip Gnosis said, shaking his head, "you guys fell for a textbook distraction."

Milcom and Belhor lowered their gazes. Madelyne took a sip of her macchiato and peeled her banana. "Did you bring some for the rest of us?" Mammon bitingly asked. Madelyne, annoyed, and realizing she couldn't quite remember how the banana and macchiato got into her hands, ignored the verbal jab.

"What exactly did the Twin Chickens do out there?" Ekron asked.

Silence.

"They launched another symmetric attack," Madelyne mumbled through her half-chewed banana.

"Another?" said Ekron.

"The first time they pulled it off was when they escaped St. Veronica's."

Ekron sighed. "So what happened from the perspective of a disillusioned worldview?"

Mammon laughed. "The monk took a ginormous shit on stage."

Everyone else groaned.

"Then what happened from the perspective of an illusioned worldview?" Ekron asked.

Madelyne swallowed her coffee. "The monk made some disparaging comments about women."

Everyone groaned again. "Damn it," said Hip Gnosis. "That's even worse."

"The monk, one of our most useful chess pieces," said Ekron, "has been captured by our opponent and removed from the board. Our play has at least revealed to us some previously unknown capabilities on the part of our competition. Madelyne..."

Madelyne looked up. Ekron pointed to the stack of five spiral-bound pamphlets. "I hope that's the report the Intelligence Unit produced on the Chickens."

Madelyne grabbed the stack. "Copies for everyone." She passed the pamphlets out. Everyone thumbed through them.

"Alegría Luz Urizar," Ekron muttered. "And Yakov Rabinowitz-Brown. These little chickens have some very interesting backstories."

Hip Gnosis broke out laughing, long and hard and loud. Everyone tensed, unsure what his mirth yet meant.

"Yes..." he finally said. "And the game is not... hold

on…" He cleared his throat, then spoke in surround sound, "THE GAME IS NOT OVER. IN FACT, FOR THE TWIN CHICKENS, IT HAS ONLY BEGUN!"

Everyone nodded silently. Hip Gnosis laughed again.

"LET'S GO EXPLOIT SOME BACKSTORIES!"

***

Jake and Joy reached for each other in the dark. Joy nestled her head into Jake's chest. He wrapped an arm around her shoulders. Disoriented, they could no longer tell if they were standing or lying down—exteroceptive and interoceptive spatial awareness had dissolved like butter in a pan of sautéed mushrooms. "Are we the pan?" Jake asked. "No." Joy giggled. "I think we're the mushrooms."

"Cute metaphor," said Jake. "I'm glad I can hear your thoughts now."

"It's a simile, and I thought it was yours. I was listening to your thoughts."

"No, I was listening to yours."

"Interesting…" they said simultaneously. Then they blinked and their vision adjusted. They were standing beside Sarah and Nimrod in the atrium of the abandoned aquarium that served as the headquarters of the Worldview Freedom Fighters. Clapping echoed. Hailee, Azrael, Levi-not-Levi, and Ponth J. Sahib, all smiles, emerged from the shadows.

"What's good?" Azrael said to Nimrod, who grinned and pulled his friend in for a pound. "Long time," said Nimrod.

Hailee and Levi-not-Levi mobbed Jake and Joy as if they were rock stars. "Oh my god," Hailee chirped. "You guys were awesomely, astonishingly, amazingly amazing!"

Ponth smiled at Sarah with an outstretched hand. "Great job out there."

"We need to talk," she responded. They stepped away from the group.

"You gonna slug me now?" said Ponth.

Sarah shook her head. "I understand now why you pushed the Chickens into the field. They needed to experience directly what it is that we do."

"And they couldn't have done it without you and Nimrod. I needed to throw you all into the fray and get you used to working together."

"I get that. But you are keeping way too many things from me."

"I'm sorry I had to keep the location of the Stakeholders close to the vest."

"Abraham is not just a Stakeholder. He's my husband."

"He's not just your husband. He's a Stakeholder."

"You trusted Nimrod with that information before me?"

"Trust wasn't the issue. Need-to-know was."

"And he needed to know before I did?"

Ponth took a breath. "When the time came for you to know, for the explicit purpose of assisting the Twin Chickens in derailing Hip Gnosis's plot to entrap the—"

"Ladee Dada."

"What?"

"Jake calls him the Ladee Dada."

"That's right, he does," Ponth said. "When you needed to know, I authorized Nimrod to take you and the Ladee Dada and the Twin Chickens to Eternity. So everyone could understand what they needed to understand, create a plan of action, and execute it. Which is what you did."

Laughter echoed through the aquarium. Ponth and Sarah looked over at the rest of the group. Jake was dancing the Macarena while Joy did the Floss. Ponth smiled. "Those two did good for a pair of broken, lost, confused little babies, huh?"

Sarah narrowed her eyes. "They did. Came up with a plan and managed to stop Hip Gnosis in the nick of time."

"Or the nicole of time." Ponth winked.

"But how'd you and the Stakeholders even know about Hip Gnosis's plan to martyr the Ladee Dada?"

Ponth sighed. "I promise. When the time is right, I will tell you."

"But not now?"

"No, Sarah. Not now."

Sarah folded her arms and drew herself to her full height

and hypotactically stated solemnly before she walked away to join the rest of the group, "You're a clever man, Ponth. Be careful you don't out clever yourself."

Ponth paratactically stared into nothingness for a moment, then he shook his head and followed, approaching the group with arms outstretched. "Guys, this is a win. A big one." Everyone clapped again. "I failed to bring some champagne or something, so let's just pretend." He raised his hand as if it contained a glass. Everyone else did the same. "To our new allies," he continued. "The Twin Chickens. I'm sorry I had to throw you into the deep end of the pool. But it was sink or swim time, and Joy, Jake, you two swam gloriously. And now you understand what we fight for. We free people. One perspect—" He paused and winked. "One perspection at a time. Hip Gnosis is an overwhelming adversary. But now with you two here… I think we finally have a chance to win this fight for good."

"Here, here!" everyone cheered, and pretended to drink from non-existent glasses. Hailee swallowed and said, "Oh wow. This is delicious." Ponth swished something in his mouth and swallowed too. "It is good," he said in shock. Everyone looked at the Twin Chickens, who chugged down their pretend glasses. "Are you guys doing this?" Sarah asked.

"Doing what?" Joy slurred. "Knocking back this Piper-Heidsieck Cuvee Brut? Shyeah." She stumbled toward Sarah. "Sorry, I had two refills while Ponth was going on and on and…" She wrapped her arms around Sarah's waist. "… I love you." Sarah put an arm around her and laughed. "Bit of a lightweight aren't you?" Joy nodded with a languid smile.

Ponth approached Jake and held out his hand. Jake shook it. "Maybe next time give us clearer commands. I thought you wanted us to kill the guy."

"Jeez, no," Ponth replied. "I thought I was pretty clear explaining you just needed to destroy his image."

"Negative. Not clear. At all."

"Hm," Ponth said. "Let's chalk it up to a miscommunication.

Next time, I'll verify all mission parameters are understood. Check?"

"Next time?" Jake asked.

"If you'll stay and fight with us."

"Still not sure I trust you, man."

Joy stumbled over and leaned on Jake. "Don't listen to him. We're in." Jake stiffened and Joy said, "Come on. How wonderfully wonderful was it seeing all those people de-hypnotized?"

"It was nice," Jake admitted. "Made me feel… useful."

"You're beyond useful," said Ponth. "You're indispensable. And in our next phase, we're gonna fight to keep as many of these de-hypnotized people from relapsing as we can. We'll need you."

"Okay." Jake nodded. "We'll take it one day at a time."

"That's all anyone can do, big guy. It's gonna be great. You two ready?"

Jake and Joy looked at each other with a smile. "No one's ever ready," Jake said.

Ponth grinned. "Then let the revolution begin."

Everyone raised their "glasses" and cheered again.

"And this time!" Joy shouted. "The revolution will not be… wait, wait…" she said to Jake, "You have to say it with me."

"Why?" he asked.

"Because!"

"You're fully capable of saying it on your own."

"God, you're no fun. Do you even know what I want to say?"

"Yes, I hear your thoughts."

"Then say it with me!"

"No."

Sarah interjected. "Just say it with her, Jake."

"Fine." Jake sighed and Joy grabbed his hand and he looked into her brown eyes with that ring of blue and knew then and there that beyond all else, beyond G_d and demigods and ideas in Eternity, he would always be true and loyal and full of faith with her, come good or not.

Joy smiled. "That was a very sweet internal monologue."

"Yeah," Jake grunted. "Well, let's say it."

They squeezed each other's hands and Joy laughed and they both shouted, "The revolution will not be…"

***

"… pasteurized!" Y shouted and clapped his hands. His voice bounced off the grimy vintage tile of the subway walls, and the commuters gave him a wide berth as they walked by on the platform.

"Take them spirals out your eyes! The revolution will not be pasteurized! The righteous have come again, they are waiting in Eternity! And Maitreya has awoken, not as the Compassionate One, but as the Compassionate Two! It takes two to tango! It takes two to make the sun and daughter hatch in the West. And I will have my task, O brothers, O sisters, to face this false knowledge and break it wide open! Wide open for the truth and the truth's face!"

Y laughed long and loud and wiped the tears from his face. Most commuters—on their way to offices, apartments, lounges, and department stores—walked by, noses turned up in disgust, turned down in pity, or set forward straight in passive neutrality.

But a few, just a few, stopped.

And a few, just a few, listened.

Jake and Joy will return in

The Amazing Twin Chicken Freedom Fighters: Book 2

ABOUT THE AUTHOR

Zephaniah Sole is the author of the critically acclaimed novel *A Crime in the Land of 7,000 Islands* (Black Spring Press). His short fiction has appeared in *Epiphany, Passages North, Collateral Journal, Gargoyle Magazine, Jacked* (Run Amok Crime, 2022), and *Romy Lives* (ABP, 2024). He is a Martha's Vineyard Institute of Creative Writing Author Fellow as well as an alum of VONA and Tin House.

www.ingramcontent.com/pod-product-compliance
Lightning Source LLC
LaVergne TN
LVHW041929070526
838199LV00051BA/2756
9798990485129